I0519557

Sweet Harmony
By

Carol Pearce Bjorlie

Sepia Books
Published by Indigo Sea Press
Winston-Salem

Sepia Books
Indigo Sea Press, LLC
302 Ricks Drive
Winston-Salem, NC 27103

First Sepia Books edition published
January, 2016
Sepia Books, Running Angel logo, and all production design are trademarks of Indigo Sea Press, used under license.

For information regarding bulk purchases of this book, digital purchase and special discounts, please contact the publisher at indigoseapress.com

Cover design by Stacy Castanedo

Manufactured in the United States of America
ISBN 978-1-63066-211-0

For voices I love,

Laura, Naomi, Rebecca, Karen, Pearce, and Jonah

Chapter One

AUGUST, 1937

The farmhouse creaked and shuddered in the wind like an old ship. Iris Andersen lay in bed with her pillow clutched to her chest. This is what pitch-black dark meant! A wild streak of lightning blazed across her windows. Iris chose this room because her father said it had the most windows. She'd never cover them with curtains! She wanted the stars and moon at night for company and the sun to get her out of bed. In Virginia she and Merry had shared a bed. Tonight, her first night in this room, her bed was cold and empty.

Another brilliant flash illuminated Merry cowering in the doorway.

"Move over," commanded Merry as she hurried to the bed and climbed in next to her big sister.

The next boom and bolt of lightning outlined little Martha Rose flying through the air, blonde braids swinging, to land on the bed where she burrowed between her sisters.

"My ears are scared!" she shouted. "That funder gonna' get me."

"Martha Rose, your imagination is bigger than you are," Iris said. "Settle down. Quit pushing!"

The three sisters lay side by side, waiting for the next crash of thunder. Iris heard a sniffle.

"Merry Columbine, is that you?" she asked.

"I'm scared," said Merry between sobs.

"Nine is too old to cry about a thunderstorm. All right, get in the middle," suggested Iris.

Merry climbed over Martha Rose and snuggled next to Iris. "I want to go home," she whispered.

"Don't say that around Daddy," cautioned Iris. "He is home."

*****

Iris lay awake while her sisters slept like spoons in a drawer. Behind her eyelids ribbons of winding roads unfolded across Virginia, West Virginia, Ohio, Indiana, Illinois, Wisconsin and finally Minnesota. No one she knew in Virginia had ever traveled this far. When their car approached farms with pig houses in Iowa, she and her sisters held their noses and rolled up the windows. They didn't care how hot it was! Her favorite memories were of traveling through West Virginia's valleys where houses were perched on bluffs, and white-steepled churches looked like scenes from a picture book.

Iris remembered the grin that took the place of her father's stern concentration.

He'd kept his strong hands on the steering wheel for over one thousand miles. He pointed to a marker that read "Harmony, The Biggest Little Town in Southern Minnesota." His gleaming red-blonde head turned from side to side as he nodded in recognition at familiar landmarks. He was coming home. Iris was leaving home. She might as well be in a foreign country. Each rotation of the car's tires pulled her further from all that was familiar in her life.

Four days ago her family had driven from their bungalow on Brook Road in Richmond, Virginia. Her grandparents stood rooted to the sidewalk, waving as the car moved away. Her best friend, Dorothy, appeared, her dark curls tangled from sleep. She gave Iris a three-page letter written in the night. Iris missed her already. Her mouth spread in a grin as she recalled the school photograph Dorothy included with her letter. Dorothy was as short as Iris was tall, and as round as Iris was thin. Iris' pale blonde hair hung below her shoulders, while Dorothy's head of dark curls was as short and springy as a poodle's.

In the back seat Iris' sisters slumped like heaps of rumpled laundry on either side of their mother, two white-blonde heads on either side of her mother's curly dark hair. Lulled by the summer heat, they slept the last miles of the journey.

Her father drove through the quiet town of Harmony, past occasional open bed trucks, the one-room post office, a towering grain elevator ("The Prairie Castle" her father called it) and a red brick church on a hill. He'd whispered, "That's where I was baptized and your Andersen grand-parents were married. The cemetery behind the church is where they are buried. You'll make new friends on Sunday, and I'll greet some old ones." He told Iris about his Sunday school teacher, Miss Catherine. He said that when she hypnotized his class of squirming twelve-year-old boys with her story of Daniel in the Lions' Den, he could feel the hot breath of those big cats on his neck.

Iris had touched his arm, pointing to a sign, "Harmony Creamery." Horace Anderson rubbed his stomach and licked his lips as if he could taste sweet cream. Iris smiled at his pantomime. She jiggled her feet in excitement. Impatience traded places with homesickness. She wanted to yell, "We're here!" After more than 1,300 miles, she could barely wait the remaining minutes until she saw her new home: a farmhouse, red barn, chicken coop and - a horse! A neighboring farmer had taken in the chickens and the Belgian workhorse when her Minnesota grandparents died within a week of each other a year ago. Her father pulled off the blacktop and onto a dirt lane.

There it stood. The white two-story farmhouse was bigger than Iris imagined. There was the red barn her father had described, the chicken house and a green tractor parked in a shed. She glanced past her mother's head through the rear window. A whirlwind of dust eddied in circles behind them. The car slowed as they passed a fence covered with pink roses, pulled around to the back of the house, then stopped.

Her father breathed a deep sigh, relaxed his grip on the steering wheel and let his hands fall to his lap. "At last," was all he said.

When he switched off the engine, Iris' mother and sisters

continued to sleep in the back seat while she and her father sat staring at the house.

Iris would never forget opening the car door and stepping out. She wanted to be the first one out of the car, the first one to step onto Minnesota's black dirt.

The farmhouse wore a recent coat of white paint. The windows were sparkling clean, long and narrow. The women at the Lutheran church her grandparents attended had come in and cleaned for her family. It was their way of saying welcome. This was the biggest house Iris had seen. A rooster weather vane swung on top of the barn's steep gray roof. Iris heard the cluck of chickens in the distance. She folded her arms across her rumpled blouse and whispered through the open car window, "Daddy, I like it."

Nine-year-old Merry Columbine rubbed her blue eyes and flipped her long hair over her shoulders as she leaned forward to see.

Martha Rose peeked through her pale bangs and asked in a groggy voice, "Mendasoda?"

Iris shouted into the car, "We made it! We're here!"

Her mother's blink and startled, "Huh!" made the girls laugh.

Still drowsy from her hot nap, Iris' mother looked out the window. The house loomed over them. Iris saw tears soften her eyes. She wondered, *Do grownups get homesick?* She looked again at her mother and smiled at her unruly black hair. After their long trip, it had tumbled from its neat bun, and hairpins stuck out from her head like antennae.

Iris' father held the house key high. "Ev-er-y-bo-dy out! This is the end of the line."

"Horace, I will never get back in that car again," Iris' mother groaned.

Iris watched her family climb out of the car on stiff legs; then she turned to study their new home. The house offered no clue to the life she would lead there. Goose bumps rose on her arms. Her thoughts were interrupted by three-year-old Martha

Rose who jumped up and clapped her hands.

"My house! My house!" she sang as she began a skipping dance around her father.

Horace Andersen tilted his head and closed his eyes; his hair gleamed in the sun.

He put his arm around Iris and said, "The smell hasn't changed a bit; the earth, the corn, everything is just the way I left it. I remember Mother picked lilacs from this bush. She opened the dining room window when they bloomed…"

"Go in," interrupted Martha Rose, bobbing and reaching for the key.

"Where's Merry?" he asked.

"Here, Daddy," answered his middle child. Merry leaned her thin body against her mother, hugging her waist with one arm. Her fair cheeks were cherry pink in the August heat.

"Come along, Laura Ellen, we're in this together." With ceremony Iris' father unlocked the door, stood aside and invited them in. "Ladies first!"

The two youngest girls raced into the kitchen, circled the large table and streamed into the dining room.

Iris stood in the kitchen with her mother and father. Horace hugged his daughter. "Well, I've brought my little girl home," he said.

"Daddy, I'm almost thirteen, remember?" Iris said, and moved out of the reach of his long arms. Her parents smiled at one another. Iris knew that smile. It meant they thought they knew more than she did.

She looked around and tried to picture her tall father as a boy seated at this kitchen table with his parents and younger brother. Most of the first floor of her little house in Virginia could fit in this room.

From the doorway Merry asked, "Daddy, where do we sleep?" She and Martha Rose held hands.

"All my girls sleep upstairs. Remember our plan? Martha Rose, mind the steps; they're steep. Your mother and I will share the bedroom next to the kitchen. Mothers and fathers have slept in that room for three generations, going on four."

Iris chuckled as her sisters scrambled up the stairs. She heard Merry shout, "Here's mine!" as she located the room with the large window that looked out over a pasture and a quiet, "Mine," from Martha Rose in the front room, followed by, "So big!"

Iris' mother took her by the hand and said, "Let's have a look at the parents' room." They walked into the echoing hall and stood in the doorway of the bedroom. Iris noticed that from the window you could see a fence covered with roses. "Oh, Iris, I hadn't expected it to be beautiful. It will be like sleeping in a garden."

Iris thought the white wallpaper of twining ivy looked messy, but if her mother liked it, that was good. Laura Ellen planned to put her tall chest of drawers in this room, along with her vanity table with the tilting mirror her grandfather had made in Virginia. The kitchen table had been here since Iris' father was a boy, and there were beds in each bedroom. Tomorrow the rest of their belongings would arrive from Virginia.

"Mother," Iris said, "You can put your hurricane lamp on a table by the door. Every time you walk past it, you'll remember Richmond." Iris knew her mother prized the kerosene lamp that had been used during the Civil War by her grandparents. There were pink roses hand-painted on the globe.

"Oh, Iris. What a good idea." Her mother squeezed Iris' hand, then touched a crumpled handkerchief to her eyes. In a bright voice she added, "Let's go up together and find your room. I believe it's at the top of the stairs."

Later that evening thunder began to rumble over the fields and wind stirred the roses along the drive. Iris lay in her bed trying to find a spot that felt right.

Her mother came into the room.

"It seems rain found us," she said as she closed the window next to Iris' bed. She sat next to Iris and kissed her daughter's forehead. "Sleep well, Sweetheart. I don't know what I would have done without your good humor on this trip. You're growing up. Martha Rose can be a trial at times, and I appreciate your patience."

Iris grinned up at her mother and said, "You mean like the time she had a scratching fight with Merry about who wanted to sit with Daddy, and he had to stop the car and threaten to leave them on the road?"

"Yes, that was one of them," said her mother.

Iris reached for her mother's arm and asked, "Mother, aren't you glad to be here at last? I can't wait 'til tomorrow. I'm going to walk over every inch of this farm. Daddy says it's 300 acres."

Her mother sighed and stood up. "It's going to take some getting used to on my part. One minute I'm excited; the next, I wonder if we were out of our minds to pick up and leave everything. Farmers are leaving Minnesota. We're fish swimming upstream." She blew Iris a kiss and switched off the bedside lamp. As she left the room, she turned and added, "I'll be honest with you, Iris. A year seems like a long time right now."

A chill settled in the pit of Iris' stomach. If her mother wondered why they had come, then why indeed? It certainly wasn't Iris' idea! Everything had been perfect the way it was. Her father was the twelfth grade English teacher at John Marshall High School. Everyone said he was the best teacher in the whole school. The next thing Iris knew, he'd convinced her mother they should return to his vacant boyhood home and start farming! Iris was ready to head back east at a moment's notice.

From Martha Rose's room, Iris heard her father say, "Good night, my little peach."

"Good night, my long tall daddy," the little girl replied. "Are you weady to hear my pwayrers?"

"Of course, Pumpkin. Go ahead."

Iris heard the creak of bedsprings as her father sat down on Martha Rose's bed.

"NowIlaymedowntosleep,IpraytheLordmysouldtokeepifIsh ouddiebeforeIwake," she took a big gulp of air, "IpraytheLordmysouldtoshake. Amen! Daddy, tomorrow I'm gonna' find me a tiny segret cubby. This house way big."

Her father chuckled and said, "I'm sure you will. There are a lot of hideaways in this old house, and I know you will discover one just your size. Sleep well, Peanut."

"I not a peanut," Martha Rose said.

The stairs squeaked as her father went downstairs.

After Martha Rose and Merry fell asleep in her bed, Iris listened as the storm moved further away and the night air cooled. She pulled the sheet up to her chin. Here she was, Iris Andersen of Richmond, Virginia, in bed in Harmony, Minnesota, more than a thousand miles from home. She cuddled close to Merry. At least the first night wasn't going to be a lonely one.

*****

Two days later Iris' family drove to the brick church they passed earlier in the week. Iris held the picture of her church in Richmond in her mind's eye. Fragrant purple wisteria vines draped from the tall pines and reached for the steeple. In the graveyard behind the church, Rebel and Yankee soldiers lay buried side by side, at peace at last. Her grandparents sat with her every Sunday morning. No two buildings could be more different than her church and this one. There were no wisteria vines, magnolia trees or a stained glass window of the Good Shepherd.

Her father led the way down the red carpet and entered a pew. The family filed in behind. When they were seated, he whispered to Iris, "This is exactly where we sat. My mother and father were bookends, with me and Luke in reaching distance. It seems the church shrank since I left." He nodded to a baldheaded man who grinned at him. Then her father stood up, waved and grinned back, pointing to his family.

"Daddy." Iris pulled on her father's suit coat. "Sit down. Everybody's looking."

The organ began to wheeze. As the processional began, the choir and congregation rose, singing, "Dearest Jesus, We Are Here." Iris rolled her eyes and punched Merry with her elbow. "That about says it all," she muttered.

After the service, Iris' father was hugged and tugged about by most of the congregation, while Laura Ellen and her girls followed like chicks. Iris noticed the girls didn't wear gloves, so she snuck hers into her mother's purse. Every person was a stranger. They even looked different: tall, thin, blonde, pale. Every time her father said, "Well, I don't believe it," when someone introduced themselves, Iris and Merry slid their eyes towards one another in their secret language, *If someone doesn't get me out of here, I will scream.*

At last the Andersens piled into the car to head home. Her father sat behind the wheel and said, "I forgot something. Everybody out."

"Oh Daddy, I'm hot!" whined Merry Columbine.

"I need all my girls," her father said. He opened the back door. Iris noticed her mother shoot him an exasperated glance. They followed him down a path that led to the rear of the church. Martha Rose held her father's hand and skipped beside him while Merry trailed behind, kicking rocks with her black patent leather shoes.

Iris muttered, "You'll ruin your new shoes, Merry Columbine."

"Will not," mumbled Merry.

"Will too," answered Iris.

"Mind your own business," her sister retorted.

Iris' mother tapped Merry on the shoulder and shook her head. Her lips were pressed together in a straight line.

Then their father announced, "Girls, your Andersen ancestors are buried right here." He stood in front of two granite grave markers. "Oh, the stories they could tell."

Iris walked up to one stone and read, "Benjamin Lars Andersen. Ragnild Olsen Anderson. My grandparents!" She knelt on the scrubby grass and traced the names with her finger.

The last time Iris had seen them was when Merry was born. There had been letters and packages for birthdays and Christmas. She was sad that she had grown up without knowing them.

Merry stooped before the other stone and read, "Kjersti Ongen Andersen, Lars Ole Andersen."

"Did you know them, Daddy?"

"These were my grandparents. Of course I knew them."

"Let's bring flowers," Merry said. "There's flowers everywhere but here."

"Let's do it," he said.

Martha Rose said, "I am gona bwing dem a pitcher of me. They can see how big I got."

Merry sighed, "You are so ridiculous, Martha Rose."

"No, I not." She flipped one braid over her shoulder.

"Ridiculous," added Merry.

"Daddy, am I?" asked Martha Rose.

"Ah, let's go home, girls," her father answered.

*****

That night when the two younger girls were in bed, Horace took three kitchen chairs out to the yard and he, Laura Ellen and Iris sat together and watched the stars appear. Horace smoked a pipe, "To keep the mosquitoes away."

"The stars are so close," said Iris' mother.

"There is nothing like a Minnesota sky," said her husband. "I can't figure out why I left this place. I guess I was a farm boy hankering to see the ocean." He looked at Iris, "You're going to love it here, Sweet Pea; I just know it."

Iris wasn't sure. Harmony was a foreign country. Even the dirt was different. In Richmond it was light and sandy near the river. Here it was black. She thought the fields looked like they'd been burned by a raging fire. The wind blew constantly.

The house was too big. From Iris' room she could see forever, into the next county probably. She did have a favorite spot: the barn with its loft and ladders. If she could stay here in the dim cool light and watch the work horse as he stood looking back at her, she'd be happy. When she left the farm, people stared at her. She was the new girl. It seemed like no one ever moved *to* Harmony.

Another thought came into her mind: was her old house lonesome for her? Do houses get lonesome? Iris missed the tangle of honeysuckle vines that grew outside her bedroom window and the heavy lemon-almond fragrance of the magnolia tree. A fig tree stood right next to the house, and in the summer wasps and honey bees buzzed all day. In Harmony on a hot afternoon, all she could smell was dust; all she could hear was the rattle of cornstalks. She let out a puff of air that shifted a straggling wisp of hair from her forehead.

She clasped her hands behind her head and gazed at the stars. The Milky Way was a powdery band in the sky. A light glowed through lace curtains her mother had brought from Richmond. *Well*, she thought, *the house looks lived in now.*

After her father's parents died from a virulent flu a year ago, the house stood empty. It faced a summer of roses, a winter of snow and a spring of tulips, lilacs and peonies alone. In 1881 Iris' great-grandparents had immigrated from Norway to homestead and farm this land. Now after a trial period of a year, if her mother and father were in agreement, her family would stay.

She deserved a say in their decision.

11

Chapter Two

SEPTEMBER

School began September seventh. Iris could not believe the color of the autumn sky. After looking up "blue" in her mother's dictionary, Iris decided this blue was cerulean. Migrating Canada geese flew high overhead in a V formation, honking and making a racket.

Iris wondered what was going on at Nathaniel Bacon Elementary School in Richmond. What would Dorothy do without her? What would she do without her best friend? This year she was supposed to start piano lessons with Mr. Bolling. Iris worried about the first day at Harmony Elementary. She'd be the new girl who talked funny.

Iris listened to herself talk now. She couldn't help it. She did sound different.

On the first day she and Merry held hands as they walked up the stone steps into the brick building. The hallways were wide. Miss Davis, the principal, stood at the double doors greeting students. She looked at Merry and Iris and said, "Well, here you are! I've been thinking about you all summer." She took Merry's hand. "Let me walk you to your room. Iris, I'll be back for you."

Iris watched as the small grey-haired woman walked Merry down to a classroom and walked in with her. About five minutes later she came back for Iris.

She didn't take Iris' hand. Iris was too old for that. Iris' classroom was the last one on the left. Miss Davis led her into the room. All the boys and girls stopped talking and looked at her. Miss Davis said, "Hello, sixth graders! This is Iris Andersen from Virginia. Isn't it wonderful to have a new friend in Harmony?"

Miss Davis had a smile as sweet as a baby's. The class said, "Hello, Iris," in unison. They must have been practicing. Mrs. Nervig, the tall, dark-haired teacher, led Iris to a desk next to a slim girl with the darkest eyes Iris had ever seen. The girl said, "Hi, I'm Julie! I'm so glad you're next to me. Do you like to read? What's your favorite book? I love to read. Madeline L'Engle is my favorite author. Maybe we can share books!"

Iris took her seat as quiet as a mouse. She did smile at Julie who was tall, even sitting down.

*****

Three weeks later during history, Iris looked up from her desk. A gray spiral towered on the horizon. Smutty wind swirled as a dark finger of cloud moved towards the school. She gasped.

Brrring, brrring! The school bell startled her. Around her the class rose to their feet in one motion and hurried to the door.

"Iris, hurry," called Julie. "We're going to the basement."

Iris left her pencil on her desk and ran to get in line. Her legs trembled as she bolted down the stairs. Questions flooded her mind. She grabbed Julie's arm and whispered, "What about my parents, my house? Suppose Martha Rose is outside!"

Julie looked at her new friend and replied, "We're safe here. This school has never been hit by a tornado, and it is so old my mother went here."

"So did my father," murmured Iris.

Her class sat on the floor against a wall in the basement. They looked at her as she stood to search for Merry's class.

Earlier that morning Iris had tried to answer their questions about the ocean. (No one in her whole class had seen the ocean.) "Well," she began. "It is cold and salty, . . . and big . . .you can't see the end of it . . . sometimes it's gray and sometimes green . . ." How could you tell someone about the ocean?

Now she would experience a tornado. She looked for

Merry's class as the lights went out. Mrs. Nervig lit a kerosene lantern and held it high as other classes began to glow in lantern light.

Julie tugged Iris to the floor, "You have to stay down. If the wind comes, put your arms over your head like this." Julie pulled her knees to her chest and crossed her arms over her head with her head bowed over her knees. Her dark hair hid her face, but Iris heard her say, "It's going to get loud, but we are safe," she repeated.

Iris didn't believe her. If they were safe, why was everyone quiet? Then Iris heard a noise like a freight train. There was a roar, a blast; then everyone's head went down. A terrible boom was followed by a violent crash. Iris felt the vibration in her spine. Her heart thumped and she put her fingers in her ears and squeezed her eyes shut. Could a person be scared to death?

Julie touched her arm and said, "That didn't sound good. My gosh, I think we're hit! Look, Mrs. Nervig's waving for you."

Iris got up and walked on rubbery legs to the bright lantern where her teacher sat. Around her boys and girls whispered excitedly.

Mrs. Nervig said, "Iris, you must be terrified. What an awful introduction to Harmony. I do wonder if you could help. I know you have young sisters at home, and you have a calm way with the little children at recess. Would you sit with the first grade while their teacher checks on her classroom? I'll send someone to help you."

"Yes, I will, Mrs. Nervig," said Iris. She hoped her act of bravery hid her shakiness.

A cluster of small children huddled together. Iris heard one child whine, "I want my mommy now!"

She sat down with them. "What are all these tears about?" she asked in a bold voice. Her mouth was dry and she wanted her own mother, but she couldn't let on that she was as scared as the first graders. "This is just a big wind and a good soaking rain," she added.

"Huh! This is not, 'just a big wind and a good soaking rain,'" a deep voice said from behind her. "I don't know where you came from, but here we respect wind."

Iris looked over her shoulder. The voice belonged to an older boy, a toasty-brown skinned Indian. At a closer glance Iris saw that he had blue eyes. Thick black bangs hung even with his eyebrows.

"My name is Oscar Runs Like Fox. Mrs. Nervig sent me to help you. Sounds like you need it."

Iris tried not to stare. "I might not know anything about tornadoes, but do you know anything about children?" she asked. "I've got little sisters and I know how to calm them."

Oscar's eyes widened. "You're the girl from Virginia! Do you talk like that always or only when you're scared?"

She stood up and put her hands on her hips. "My accent is as real as yours," she shot back.

Oscar stood up in one smooth movement and walked away.

Iris' temper had gotten the best of her again. She talked first and thought second.

Another bell sounded and Iris' class returned to their room. She wanted to ask Julie about the Indian boy with blue eyes, but one look at her room and all other thoughts blew away like the wind that swept through their school. An oak tree was tossed against the side of the building. Branches protruded into her classroom, and rain streamed onto the floor. Papers blew about and glass crunched underfoot. Following her teacher's directions, Iris collected her sweater and lunch box from the cloakroom behind the sliding blackboard and joined the other children on the front steps of the school. They would wait for their parents there. Her lunch box rattled in her hands.

Iris spotted Merry and motioned her over. How would their father get here? She wanted to be home right now and know that Martha Rose and her mother were safe. Then she saw their workhorse, Joshua, approaching. Her father sat hunched under an oilcloth poncho. Rain poured from his back onto the horse.

Iris' heart pounded as she walked out to meet him. Most of

her class sat on the steps, protected from the rain and wind by the overhanging roof. How would she and Merry get up on the back of that enormous horse? Everyone was watching.

As her father reached down a hand to help her, she heard a familiar voice at her side, "I'll give you a leg up." Oscar Runs Like Fox held his hands cupped to form a step. Iris put a foot into his outstretched hands, grabbed her father's arm and up she went onto Joshua's back behind her father. Oscar lifted Merry up to sit behind her. "Hold tight," was all he said.

As Iris turned to thank him, he ran to join a man who rode a pinto pony. The boy with the blue eyes grabbed the man's hand, and in a blink he swung up and they rode away. The pony had not even stopped.

Her sister clutched her waist until Iris complained, "Merry Columbine, you're about to squeeze my guts out!"

Merry began to cry.

Rain from her father's poncho dripped onto her arms as she circled his waist. Joshua started his slow walk. Iris, huddled behind her father, asked, "Daddy, is everything all right? Mother? Martha Rose? What about the house?"

He answered, "We're fine. Your school took a real beating. It's a good thing your mother didn't see that!" Her father turned his head and nodded at the old building.

Iris looked back. A section of the roof had blown away. The tree that now leaned against her classroom had been ripped from the ground, roots and all, from across the street. Rain pounded them, and the wind carried twigs and leaves in the air.

"We won't have to go to school tomorrow," she said. Her next thought was that she would miss her friend Julie and fleeting glimpses of the boy named Oscar.

"My guess is you'll have quite a holiday," said her father. "The electricity is out all over the county. We'll be eating by candlelight."

"Daddy, what about the corn and wheat?" asked Iris.

Her father's voice was grim. "It was about ready to harvest, but we've lost it all."

16

The threesome continued their plodding journey. Trees looked like a giant hand had twisted the tops off. Crops were flattened and lay in pools of water. Cornstalks and tree limbs littered the road.

"Daddy, are you sure Mother and Martha Rose are all right?" she asked.

"A little scared, but they're fine," he reassured her. "Your little sister spent the morning whirling and twirling around the yard, making herself dizzy, saying, 'Look at me, look at me! I am the big big wind!' When I finally did look at her, there it was on the horizon, a black and ugly tower of storm headed straight for us. I grabbed her and ran into the house, took your mother by the hand and we tore down those basement steps. It was like Martha Rose knew . . ."

Iris thought he sounded thrilled at the adventure.

"I had forgotten how violent Minnesota's weather can be." As an afterthought, he added, "Your mother's worked herself into a real state."

Then Iris saw their house. It stood out against the purple-black sky and faced the wind like a Viking ship. A trembling sigh shook her chest, and her tears of relief were disguised by the rain.

*****

A week later when Iris was beating a rug on the clothesline, a dark Ford rambled down the lane. It stopped and a man got out and greeted her, "Good afternoon, young lady. Is your mother at home? My name is Ivan Strugatsky and I'm the Watkins man."

Iris watched as he took a black case from the trunk of his car. She thought he must be a doctor. She folded the rug over her arm. "I'm Iris Andersen," she said. "Mother's inside. Why don't you come in?" She led the way into the kitchen where her mother stood at the sink peeling potatoes. "Mother, this is the Watkins man," she said.

"Oh, hello, Mr. Watkins," her mother said, wiping her

17

damp hands on her apron.

The visitor laughed and Iris liked the way the corners of his eyes crinkled. "My name is Ivan Strugatsky, and I sell Watkins' products 'from the store to your door.'" He patted the case at his side and leaned over to unlatch it.

Iris' father came in from the barn, and she pulled him over to their visitor. "Daddy, this is the Watkins man," she said. "Mr. Stru-gat-sky."

Her father shook hands with the salesman. "Oh, do I remember the Watkins man! Laura Ellen, you will be amazed at the stuff he has in that case!" Her father took off his jacket and work gloves and settled back in a kitchen chair. Iris leaned against him and peered into the satchel. It was crowded with jars and tins and packets of every size and shape. It was a treasure chest!

"Take a look, Mrs. Andersen," said Mr. Strugatsky. He held up a brown bottle. "This is our best-selling kitchen item: Watkins Vanilla, eight ounces for fifty cents. With Thanksgiving and Christmas around the corner, I know you'll need some fresh nutmeg, and pie spices, cinnamon. . ."

Martha Rose came into the kitchen and made straight for the opened case of goods. "What is that?" she interrupted.

"I have anything you need, little Missy," said Mr. Strugatsky. He smiled so broadly that this time his eyes disappeared entirely.

Iris giggled.

"Here's a stick of gum for you and your sister," he handed Martha Rose two paper-wrapped sticks of gum.

"We have another tister uptairs," said the little girl.

"Well, here's one for her too," said the peddler, handing over one more red-wrapped stick. He continued to take small parcels out of the case. "Now here we have horehound drops for winter coughs, castile shampoo for the lady, and," he took out a big bottle, "brown liniment, good for man or beast. We have mouthwash, headache powders, tooth paste . . ."

Iris' eyes squinted as she peered into the case. There was a red-and-black striped can of Watkins Petro-Carbo Salve and a bottle of Lemon Rinse for Hair that Shines like the Sun.

"Mother, do you think we could buy some lemon rinse," asked Iris, "and some horehound drops? And look, pudding mix."

Martha Rose added, "And more!"

"Girls, girls," their father began, "hold back. It's not Christmas. Well, sir," he said, "I can use one bottle of that Brown liniment for our old horses' legs and horehound drops for the girls. I'm afraid that's it for today. Our feet aren't on the ground yet, if you know what I mean. That tornado set us back."

Iris watched her father's helpless shrug, and she turned her head. Her mother twisted her apron in her hands.

Mr. Strugatsky took out the bottle of liniment and a sack of cough drops and put them on the kitchen table and snapped the case shut. "I understand perfectly," he said. "I look forward to seeing how you get along here when I return." He shook hands one more time with Iris' father. "Your folks were the salt of the earth, Mr. Andersen. I miss them. It's good to see the family home again."

"Thank you for your kind words," said Iris' father. He stepped into the backyard to see the Watkins man off.

After Mr. Strugatsky left, Iris went upstairs to her room. She closed her door, sat on the edge of her bed and picked at a hangnail with her teeth. She thought about her father's words. What had he meant by "not on our feet yet," and being "set back"?

Were they going to be poor? In Virginia she and her mother used to dress up, wear gloves and hats and take the street car to town to buy hand cream. They weren't rich, but they always stopped for a treat at the ice cream parlor before they went home. She couldn't remember the last time she had been to a real store. In her opinion, there wasn't a real store in Harmony. Downtown consisted of a bank, a shoemaker, a hardware store, a junk store, the Vandheim-Landy Pharmacy and the Harmony

Farmer Store Grocery that also sold ladies stockings and a few hats.

Twice this fall she'd helped her mother can green beans and tomatoes from nearby farms. The ladies' circle from the church brought welcome baskets of bread and butter pickles and tangy sauerkraut, plus a hundred pound sack of potatoes. Iris hadn't thought of these things as charity. Were they? Life was different here. She heard a distant train whistle. Maybe it was headed east.

Chapter Three

OCTOBER

Iris usually woke startled, disoriented, her heart beating hard in her chest, but when she opened her eyes this morning, she knew where she was.

Yesterday her mother opened their blanket chest and brought out quilts. Iris' favorite was a faded Star of Bethlehem made from dress scraps her Richmond grandmother had saved. Her mother pointed out the fabric of pink Sunday dresses and flowered nightgowns she wore as a girl.

This morning Iris' quilt was pulled up to her nose. She was curled on her side, her feet tucked under her. She faced her dim window and wondered, *Isn't this a school day?* Her mother hadn't called to wake her. She saw her sweater and blue plaid skirt laid out on a chair. Iris pulled the quilt from her head. She smelled the lavender sprigs her mother scattered over the linen closet shelves.

She peeked out from under her covers and studied the window. SNOW! In a heartbeat she was awake and on her knees. She jumped out of bed and pressed her face against the freezing window pane. Snow whirled sideways in the wind, then flew straight up. Flakes flurried and blotted the sky. Snow in Virginia had never done tricks! The few snows Iris had seen floated down in big wet flakes.

She jumped out of bed and ran across the hall to Merry's bedroom. The icy floor shocked her feet. Merry slept peacefully on her back, as if she were floating, her braids over her shoulders.

Iris cupped her hand to her sister's ear and whispered the magic word, "Snow." Merry didn't budge.

Next she raced to Martha Rose's room. The three-year-old's rear end stuck up in the air. Iris crept over to the bedside and whispered to her in a singsong voice, "Martha Rosie Posie."

Martha Rose flattened out, rubbed her nose on her pillow and opened her eyes. Little pieces of ice clinked against the window. She sat up, her mouth a perfect O, her eyebrows arched to meet her bangs. "Get Merry," she hollered as she slipped from under her quilt.

The two girls raced into Merry's room laughing and pointing at the window. Together they leaped on her bed.

"The sky is falling; the sky is falling," shouted Iris.

"Is goose fedders, goose fedders," shrilled Martha Rose.

Still in their nightgowns, the three girls tumbled together in a hurry to get downstairs. Their mother stood at the sink and stared at the scene before her.

"Look, girls, we've moved to dreamland," she said.

Iris saw her father shoveling a path to the barn. He looked up and waved. He must have started the cozy fire in the kitchen fireplace early this morning.

Their mother said, "Oatmeal's hot. As soon as you've eaten, you can dress and go outside. Your father has been out since dawn. He says he's working. *I* say he's playing!"

The girls gulped their oatmeal and ran to get dressed. Merry was the first one downstairs. She stood in the doorway to the back porch and held out a red glove. Two puffy flakes fell on it and she blew them off.

"Eat 'em," shouted Martha Rose who pushed past Merry and stood with her mouth open to the sky, her tongue sticking out. "Ah . . . look, Mama, the snow is falling down my froat."

"Go upstairs and bring your clothes down. I'll help you dress by the fire; then we can get your coat and gloves and you can go out," said her mother.

Iris raced upstairs to get dressed.

The three girls stood in the snow on the back steps, their hands outstretched to catch the flakes.

Their father came around the barn with a grin on his face.

He hugged Iris to him. "Here are my snow maidens at last," he exclaimed. He pulled a long wooden sled. As Iris stepped out into the snow, he called, "Hop on!"

Iris sat down and held on tight as he whirled her down the drive. He ran fast, and at the turn, the centrifugal force nearly whipped her off the sled. "Ya-hoo!" she shouted in her best Rebel yell.

Her father shouted back, "Ya-hoo!"

Iris jumped off and called, "Merry, you're next," and laughed as her sister's braids flew out behind her.

When Martha Rose finished her ride, the little girl patted her face with her mittens and proclaimed, "My nose done froze."

Iris and her sisters stomped the little hill near the kitchen garden to pack the snow until it was glossy slick. They swept down it crowded together on the sled. Their mother came for a short time with a large cookie sheet that was just Martha Rose's size. Iris begged her mother, "Go down once, Mother, just once," but Laura Ellen refused.

At noon the girls' mother called her family in for lunch. They ate potato soup with sausage, and the hot chocolate she served declared this was a special day.

Iris asked, "Daddy, how long will the snow last?"

Her mother interrupted, "It will be there after lunch and your coats have dried," then she looked at her husband and asked, "Horace, how long will the snow last?"

He replied, "Until April. Sometimes we get snow in May."

Laura Ellen gasped and sank back into her chair.

"Let's make a snow fort," declared Iris.

"I'm going to make my first snow angel," said Merry.

"I gonna' eat it," Martha Rose added with a chocolate grin.

*****

The snow fell all day. Dusk came early and Iris and her sisters trudged indoors. At dinner Laura Ellen passed around fresh chicken potpie and Iris' favorite, rhubarb cobbler. Iris said, "Maybe it will snow on my birthday, and I won't have to go to school!" Her birthday was October twenty-fourth, two weeks away.

After their baths, Iris led her sisters downstairs where her father made a fire in the living room fireplace. Laura Ellen wrapped Martha Rose in an afghan and sat with her in the rocker. Iris knelt by the fireplace and popped corn. While they munched, Merry asked her father, "Daddy, this a good night for the naming story!"

Her father smiled at her, "You girls love stories about yourselves, and that's a fact!" He motioned for Merry to join him on the sofa and began, "Once upon a time, there was a Southern beauty who won me with her buttermilk biscuits and her sweet smile. I courted that smile and those biscuits for a year. Finally I summoned the courage to propose marriage, and she said . . . ."

"Yes!" shouted Martha Rose on cue.

"We lived in a small house on a hill in Richmond, where your dear daddy taught school. Before you could holler 'Jack Rabbit,' a baby girl joined us and we were a family. I took one look at our precious baby, and she took one look at me, and it was love at first sight. Her eyes were lavender and I said to her mother, 'This has to be . . .'"

"Iris," said Iris, grinning.

"Three years later," he continued, "there was another baby girl. When she gave me her lopsided grin, she looked like a happy little elf, so I said, 'Why, hello . . .'"

"Merry," chimed in the daughter nestled at his side.

"Yes, and 'Columbine' because your eyes are as blue as the flowers that grew in our garden. Well, time flew by, and six years later . . . I remember it like yesterday, I took my two big girls in my arms and told them about their new sister. I told them that she was perfect and pink as a . . ."

"Wose!" chirped Martha Rose proudly.

"Yes, and you are named Martha after your mother's mother, your grandmother. End of the naming story. Amen."

"But, Daddy," Iris asked, "What if we'd been boys?"

"Oh, well, I've got a name saved for a boy." He winked at his wife. "My father's name was Benjamin. I think that's a fine name for a boy, don't you? Benjamin. . . . . "

"I'm gonna' haf a brudder Benjermen," cried Martha Rose.

"Let's not get ahead of ourselves," said her mother.

"I not gettin' a head. I gettin' a brudder!" said Martha Rose.

*****

The next morning, Iris looked out of her window. Her father's path to the barn had disappeared under fresh snow. She dressed quickly and met Martha Rose at the breakfast table.

Martha Rose pulled at the neck of her sweater, "Scratchidy," she complained.

Iris heard the scrape of the snow shovel as her father cleared a drift from the back door.

She helped her little sister dress, tucking a scarf over her chest before she buttoned her coat, and tugging on warm mittens. She topped Martha Rose's blonde head with a snug wool hat. Then she put on her own coat, scarf and gloves, stuffed her pony tail under her hat, and they went outside.

"Oh, dear, where's my cookie pan?" Martha Rose asked her father.

"Martha Rose," answered her father, "things get lost for a whole winter if you don't put them in a safe place. We used to lose things in October and not find them until May." He pointed to the cookie sheet propped against the house.

Iris wondered where Merry was. Her sister would miss some good sledding. It had snowed all night. Iris went to the kitchen door. Her mother was brushing muffin crumbs from the table into her hand for the chickens. Iris saw Merry in the doorway to the kitchen, her face a shining red mask. Merry swayed and reached for the doorjamb. Iris rushed in and reached her before she fell.

"Merry!" she cried. Merry's cornflower blue eyes fluttered, swimming in tears.

"Want Mommy," she whispered, holding her throat.

Laura Ellen hurried to Merry, picked her up and carried her to the living room sofa. "You're hot as blazes," she said. "I'm going to call Dr. Brenna straight away. Iris, get your father."

Iris ran from the house. She pushed through the snow and followed her father's path to the barn. Inside he and Martha Rose were feeding Joshua. "Daddy, Mother says come! Merry is burning up." Iris could hear her voice rise higher and louder.

Her father muttered, "A tornado, a blizzard and now a sick child. Dr. Brenna will never get here." He turned to his girls, "All right, let's go in the house, and no, Martha Rose, you can't stay in the barn. The very last thing we need is to have you wander off."

Indoors Horace went to Merry's side. He put his hand on her forehead and turned to his wife.

Laura Ellen said, "I tried to phone Dr. Brenna, but the line is dead."

Iris and Martha Rose looked in from the kitchen doorway.

"I'll have to saddle Joshua and get him," their father said. "The car wouldn't get to the road." He buttoned his heavy coat, wrapped his face in his scarf until all that was visible was his eyes, then pulled on his hat with earflaps and mittens and rushed into the swirling snow.

Iris stood at the window as her father disappeared behind a curtain of thick flakes. A dull ache settled in the pit of her stomach.

Iris watched all morning as her mother sat beside her sleeping sister. She worried about her father and Joshua and about Merry, motionless on the sofa. Her mother wouldn't let them in the room in case their sister was contagious.

Martha Rose needed entertaining. She and Iris dressed and undressed every doll in the house, took their temperatures and put them to bed. They went to the window often, hoping to see their father and the doctor return from town. A deep rumble sounded as snow fell from the kitchen roof and covered the path at the back door. No one could get in or out that way now.

Iris lit a kerosene lantern and two candles to ward off the gray light that loomed outside.

In the afternoon two solemn girls sat at the kitchen table where they sipped tea and watched their mother as she went from the sink to the sofa with a cool cloth for Merry's head, then fresh sheets and a fresh nightgown.

At last there was a loud stamping on the front porch. Both girls hurried towards the living room, but their mother stopped them from entering. "You must stay away from your sister." She opened the front door. In walked a small bundle of a person, followed by their father.

"Laura Ellen, you must be so worried," he began. "You must have thought I fell in a ditch!"

All eyes were on the person who preceded him into the house.

He added, "We couldn't get in the back way, so we came in the front! I got turned around going to town, couldn't see my hand in front of my face, and then smelled smoke from a chimney and followed it 'til I came to the cabin of Laughing Sky." He shook off his coat and hugged his wife. "I went off to find the doctor and found an Ojibway healing woman practically in our back yard! This is Laughing Sky."

The family was transfixed. A thick blanket, then a coat were removed and a bright woven scarf unwound. Underneath was a small young woman with a thick black braid over her shoulder. She went straight to Merry and took the child's hand in hers.

"She's a In-di-en!" Martha Rose said breathlessly.

"Hush!" whispered Iris.

The healing woman looked up from Merry and said, "I have seen this butterfly-pattern rash on children's faces at the reservation. This is the sign of scarlet fever. We must work quickly. Mrs. Andersen, would you run a tub of cool water?"

Iris' mother looked over her shoulder at her husband as she hurried to the bathroom, her eyes full of questions. Laughing Sky lifted Merry's limp body in her arms and followed.

Merry's hair hung down like frayed ropes.

That night Horace tucked his two healthy girls into Iris' bed. They dozed through the night, listening to the murmur of adult voices. Iris heard her father go out in the night to feed Joshua. The wind howled and she shivered under her covers. The inside of her windows was covered with ice.

Later she woke and smelled coffee. Her room was as black as a well. She dozed again, thinking about Merry's feverish face and her own birthday. She couldn't help it. In two weeks she'd be a teenager.

In the morning the house was silent. Iris and Martha Rose crept downstairs and peeked into the living room. Their mother slept, covered by a blanket in a big chair next to the sofa. Iris watched until she saw Merry's narrow chest lift and fall in even breaths.

She still had the scarlet rash on her cheeks.

In the kitchen the Indian woman was at the stove and turned to greet them.

"*Aneen*! This is a good morning. Your sister is sleeping a healthy sleep."

The two girls looked her over.

"*Aneen* means hello in Ojibway," the woman explained.

"Are you an In-di-an doctor?" asked Iris.

"I am a healing women, Nuh-nuhd-duh-yey-yay-Ehkway. My mother, and her mother before her, passed on the knowledge of nature's remedies and prayers that help sick people get better."

"Did you pway?" asked Martha Rose.

"I did," replied the woman. "I prayed to the Great Spirit to help me restore health to your sister."

"Is the Great Spirit God?" questioned Iris.

"To me He is," answered Laughing Sky.

"What 'cha got?" asked Martha Rose, pointing to a pale leather pouch that hung on the back of a kitchen chair.

"This is my medicine bag." Laughing Sky opened the drawstring mouth of the bag and lifted out a smaller bag that fit into Iris' palm. "Smell," said the medicine woman.

Iris peered into the bag, then lifted the tiny sack to her nose and took a deep whiff. "Ummm, flowers," she said.

"Yes, chamomile. If I make tea from this, it will calm your sister and help her sleep. Now take a sniff of this." Laughing Sky held out another bag which Iris opened.

"Phew! That's awful." Iris handed the open bag to Martha Rose who held her nose and backed away.

Laughing Sky explained, "This is from the bark of the juniper tree, the best cure for coughs I know."

"I hope I don't get a caught," said Martha Rose.

"I hope you don't either." Laughing Sky looked closely at Martha Rose. She knelt before her. "You are a soothsayer," She turned to Iris, "And you, you are The Bold One."

Martha Rose asked, "Why am I a tooth-saver?"

Laughing Sky laughed and smoothed a blonde strand out of Martha Rose's face, "A soothsayer is a person with a special gift," she explained. "You can foretell what others cannot imagine." The woman's eyes shone like polished rocks. She touched Martha Rose's temple with her brown finger. "Your mind soars."

"I know it," whispered Martha Rose.

*****

Ever since Merry got sick, Iris hadn't slept well. Two weeks later she woke early, but this time she was anticipating her special day. Thirteen!

She slipped on her soft slippers and bathrobe and headed downstairs. All was quiet. Merry still slept on the sofa. Her mother wanted her close at night. Merry was too weak to climb stairs.

There was no mother, father or little sister in the kitchen. No cake in the oven. No card at her place at the table, no gifts. The family had forgotten her birthday. Of course they had! Merry was still terribly sick. They'd had a blizzard. No one could get to town, and the postman couldn't get to their house.

29

Iris muttered under her breath, "O, spit!"

Then the door to her mother and father's room opened and a big "Surprise!" greeted her.

Merry opened her eyes and from the sofa called, "I was just pretending to be asleep! Happy birthday, Iris!"

Her parents hugged her, and Martha Rose grabbed her hands and swung them hard. "We made a surprise for you!" she shouted.

And they had. In the oven was an enormous platter of scrambled eggs, bacon, and muffins. At Iris' place were homemade cards (three from Martha Rose) decorated with bits of ribbon and dried flowers.

And there *were* presents: a prayer book from her father that had belonged to his mother, a silver bracelet from her mother that she had worn as a girl and Martha Rose had made a decorated display of pine cones and straw.

Her mother said, "This may be the strangest birthday ever. We couldn't get to town for gifts, and I know Grandma has sent a gift which will come sometime. We just had to make do."

Her father began, "Happy Birthday to You," as her mother set a candle in the center of Iris' corn muffin.

Chapter Four

NOVEMBER

"I am sick, sick, sick, sick of this weather! I'm sick of mittens and two pairs of socks, boots, my hair mashed flat from a stupid hat and these dumb leggings!" Iris unwrapped her scarf, tossed her wool cap on the kitchen table and flung her coat over a chair by the stove. She unbuckled her boots, kicking them in a pile by the door. She flopped into a chair next to Merry, who was wrapped in a blanket drinking chamomile tea. Her mother stood at the table preparing to roll out a pie crust.

"You won't believe the awful ride home. Our bus driver is sick, and the new bus driver almost slid off the road. The back of the bus was swinging like a fish tail. It was cold, and we sat on the side of the road forever, and then he got his nerves back and kept going. It is solid ice out there! It's only November!"

Iris reached into her canvas book bag and pulled out a stack of letters. "For you," she said as she slapped them on the table in front of Merry, who let them lay there.

"Aren't you going to read them? They're from your class. All day long I hear, 'How's Merry? When's she coming back?'" Iris kicked Merry's chair leg. "When you got sick, you became everybody's *best* friend. Julie drew you a picture! Oscar says he hopes you get better." Iris placed her hands over her heart.

Two tears slid down Merry's pale cheeks. In silence she gathered her blanket around her and walked out of the kitchen. She lay down on the sofa with her face towards the wall.

Iris dropped her head and peeked sideways at her mother. Laura Ellen stood with her hands on her hips glaring at her...

Iris said, "I'm sorry . . ."

31

Her mother interrupted her, "Well! Don't tell me!" She hit the back of a chair with her rolling pin. It made a terrible cr-rack. "Iris, do you know how Merry waits for you to come home, how she looks forward to seeing you walk in the door? Sometimes I wonder if her fever will ever stay down. She's pale as milk and thin as a stick."

Iris hung her head and sniffed, "Mother, it is two degrees out there—below zero!"

"And you are lucky to be able to be out there," her mother shouted. Then in one quick motion, Laura Ellen sat down in a chair, put her head on her arms on the table and began to cry.

Iris was shocked by her mother's tone of voice. She was not a shouter. Iris brought out the worst in everyone. Her mother's shoulders began to shake with her sobs.

"Mother, Mother, really, I am sorry." Iris got up and stood behind her, "I didn't mean to make *you* cry." She put a hand on her mother's back. "Please?"

Laura Ellen pulled Iris close with one arm and continued to cry.

"You, know, Thanksgiving will be here soon. Then I'll be home all day to help. I'll do my chores, and Merry's too, and stay inside and cut out doll dresses with Martha Rose and Merry all day."

Her mother lifted her head, "Thanksgiving! Thanksgiving? Dear God, forgive me if I forget Thanksgiving this year." She stood up, took off her apron and threw it in Iris' lap. "I can't do one more thing," she said.

Iris' mother began to pace the kitchen, talking as if Iris weren't there. Her disheveled black hair framed her pale face. "I know what I'll do," her mother muttered to herself. "I'm going to pack my bags. I'm going to Virginia where I belong! I'll bed down in Mother's spare room, read a book or two, drink tea in the afternoon, visit my friends, go to *my* church." She took off her apron, handed it to Iris, stalked out of the kitchen to her bedroom and shut the door.

Iris stood with the apron in her arms. She heard her mother

opening and closing drawers, then . . . stillness. In a daze Iris picked up the ball of pie dough, rolled it in a circle and laid it in the waiting pie plate. A jar of canned apples was on the table. She poured them into the crust, sprinkling sugar and cinnamon on it the way she'd seen her mother do and began to roll out the remaining dough. She patted it and placed it on the floury bread board, pressed it down with the heels of her hands and then began to roll it out.

Merry must be sleeping in the living room. Where was Martha Rose? Oh, yes, in the barn with her father. The house was too quiet.

When Iris thought the circle of dough was thin enough, she placed it on top of the apple filling. She squeezed the edges of the crust together to keep the juices from leaking. She pricked the letter A on top for apple . . . or Andersen. She slid the heavy pie plate into the wood stove's oven and closed the door.

Would her mother really leave? She couldn't. She just couldn't. What would her father say? Her mother needed help. Iris got her coat and scarf and went to do her outdoor chores. She unlatched the chicken house door and filled the feeder with corn.

Miss Chick, Thumbelina, Sweetie Pie, Gretel and Puffy greeted her with clacking murmurs as they sat on their nests. Iris felt under each chicken for eggs and carefully placed two in her coat pocket. Her daddy said they wouldn't get many eggs in winter.

The big rooster, Sam, watched from his cage as he strutted about his kingdom. Martha Rose threatened to kill the big bird. "He wooks at me!" she declared. Once he pecked her on the leg, leaving a nasty bruise. "I'm gonna' kill dat chickum!" she howled. Iris hurried back to the house.

Iris sat at the kitchen table and looked around. Her mother was a neat person. Well, except for her hair. But since Merry had been so sick, the kitchen looked like it needed a magic broom. Iris got up, took the broom from beside the fireplace and began to brush cobwebs from under the stove and in the corners. Then she gave the floor a good sweep. She was surprised at the small mound of dust, crumbs and dirt that accumulated. Next she got the dust rag and went into the living room. Every table had a fine layer of dust. She took care of that.

Next she crept to her mother's bedroom door and listened for sounds of packing. All was silent. She opened the door a crack and peeked inside. Her mother was asleep on top of the quilt, her arms thrown wide, as if she'd flung herself down. Iris took an afghan from the bedside chair and covered her mother with it. She stood a minute and watched her mother sleep. Her hair was a mess; the curls loosened from their bun swarmed around her face. She was as beautiful as a doll.

Iris returned to the kitchen table, where she sat with her chin in her hand for several minutes. Could winter drive her mother to take the train home? Iris could hardly blame her. It was her job to change her mother's mind. She began to form a plan. When Martha Rose and her father came in from the barn, she would enlist their assistance.

Her mother slept all the dark winter afternoon. When Merry woke, her father made a fire in the fireplace; and Iris listened from the kitchen as Martha Rose kept the invalid company with stories of barn mice and sliding down hay bales in the loft. When Iris took Merry's temperature, she felt a knot of worry when it read 101 degrees. Merry's cheeks were a rosy pink. She imagined her mother taking Merry's temperature, feeling her forehead, her hot cheeks. Her mother was plain worn out with worry.

Iris looked out the kitchen window as she washed the bowl her mother had made the crust in. The pie steamed on the kitchen table. A light snow had begun to fall. As planned, Iris' father took a cup of hot tea to her mother's door. He knocked— "Laura Ellen?"—and opened the door a crack. Iris stood by his side. He said, "It's dinner time. We have a surprise for you."

"Dinner time?" Her mother yawned and sat up. "Dinner time!" she repeated. She put her hands to her head to pat her hair in place, then leaned over and put on her shoes. "How long was I asleep?"

Iris answered, "It doesn't matter."

Her father opened the bedroom door so her mother could see the dining room. The white company cloth was on the table, and the candles were lit. Martha Rose had made a centerpiece of pine cones. Merry sat in her robe at her regular place at the table, and Iris' father and Martha Rose stood waiting at their places.

Laura Ellen walked over to the table. "I don't believe it," she said. Horace put his arm around his wife's shoulder.

Iris spoke, "Before Daddy says the blessing, Mother, I want to tell you and Merry I'm sorry. Merry, I'm sorry I was cross when I got home. You looked so cozy here, and I guess I was jealous. Mother, I'm so sorry I made you cry. I'll never make you cry again. I didn't know what to do, so I fixed supper."

Her mother's smile was shy. "Well, I'm not sure I deserve all this attention, but it is nice to be treated like company. Iris, I do know you're sorry." Laura Ellen looked across the table at her husband and each of her girls and said, "I want you all to know that I'm not going anywhere!"

"Amen!" said Martha Rose.

"Amen, indeed," answered her father.

The Andersen family ate by candle light. Iris and her father had made boiled potatoes and opened a jar of canned green beans. Horace sliced a ham. The apple pie was a hit, and Iris' mother complimented her on the crust.

After dinner, Iris' mother got up to clear the table. Iris stopped her by saying, "Sit by the fire with Merry, Mother. Martha Rose and Daddy and I are going to clear and do the dishes. From now on Tuesday is your night off. We'll cook for you."

Laura Ellen turned to her husband who nodded, and said, "This was Iris' idea, but it was about time we gave you a hand. I get help with the outdoor chores, but you've been inside with a sick child. We're going to give you a rest."

Carol Pearce Bjorlie

Laura Ellen went into the living room and relaxed in the rocker. "I have the nicest family in all of snowy Minnesota. Dinner was wonderful. Iris, if tonight was an example, you'll make a fine Tuesday night cook."

Iris grinned at her father, "Daddy almost burned to potatoes."

"Now, now, don't tell my secrets and I won't tell yours," he replied. "We both have a lot to learn. There is one matter to settle," he continued. "We will not make a fuss over Thanksgiving this year. Let's be grateful to be together and eat pancakes or something highly irregular. Laura Ellen, I don't want you drowning in cranberry sauce and gravy this year."

Merry sat up on the sofa. "I'm going to get well for Thanksgiving. I just know it. Then, Mommy, you won't have to take my temperature. Soon I'm going to climb those stairs and sleep in my own bed."

"That would give me something to be thankful for," said her mother.

"And . . . " began Martha Rose, "if we have pancakes, we will have Tansgiving breakfust."

Iris brightened. "And we can eat in our pajamas," she said.

"And hope no one decides to visit," added their father.

*****

On a bright cold Thanksgiving morning, Iris and Merry set the table with their grandmother's lace cloth and put out the best china. Each plate had real gold around the edge, and in the center was a nosegay of tiny pastel flowers. There were only five plates and two cups and saucers. When they had company, Iris' mother added their own plain white dishes. Tonight looked perfect because there were enough beautiful plates for them all.

Next Merry had folded white cloth napkins at every place, and Iris lit the candles. Horace came in with a platter of sausages, and Martha Rose brought in a pitcher of warm brown sugar syrup. Iris served hot applesauce with cinnamon and her mother's favorite, buttermilk pancakes.

36

The family pulled out their chairs and sat down. Iris laughed out loud, "Daddy! You could at least comb your hair."

Horace's hair stood up in spikes on his head. "If we can wear our pajamas, I figured I didn't have to spruce up." Her father looked relaxed in his slippers and blue plaid bathrobe. "This is a first! I'm looking forward to a good game of Scrabble after breakfast, then a nap, maybe a snowball fight, then a nap, then a little soup, then a nap . . ."

"Daddy," cried Martha Rose, "Do I haf' to sleep too? I want to play in the barn. Let's slide down the hay."

Her father looked at his youngest. "You're not supposed to tell about sliding down the hay."

"Her mother shook her head and reassured her youngest child, "Your daddy's teasing, Martha Rose. I'm sure he will play in the barn, as long as you stay out of the loft! You know your daddy can't idle away a whole day. I've never known him to take a nap."

"Oh, really," said her husband, one eyebrow raised. "Just you watch. I'm taking the day off! Iris can take care of Joshua and the chickens. I am going to lead a life of leisure and be thankful for it. I expect you to do the same."

Laura Ellen said, "We can't do this every year, you know. My family has standards, and we're going to keep them. Maybe we can have company next year, you know, a real Thanksgiving."

"I'll write brother Luke in Bemidji. For now let's enjoy this one," said Horace.

Merry spoke up. "I know you're all glad to have nothing to do but sleep and go around in your pajamas all day, but I'm almost well, and I want to get dressed. I can't wait to go back to school."

"I can't believe you said that," added Iris.

Chapter Five

DECEMBER

Early in the the second week of December the family gathered at the table for breakfast. There was a knock at the door, and Iris opened it for Laughing Sky. Laura Ellen looked up from her coffee in surprise. Iris admitted, "Mother, we've planned a surprise." Her mother had a blank expression on her face. Iris continued, "Laughing Sky is going to stay with us while you and Daddy go into Rochester to Christmas shop."

Iris' mother opened her mouth to protest, but Horace came to her, untied her apron strings, and said, "Don't waste your breath trying to talk us out of this. You and I have the day to ourselves, and I can't remember the last time, can you? Get your boots on and let's go."

"Well," Iris' mother said, pushing her chair back from the table. "Horace, I've read your mother's Scandinavian cookbooks and thought I'd like to try some recipes. I didn't know how I could get the ingredients, almonds, for example, but now I can. Let's have a Norwegian celebration the way your family did."

"We better take the cookbooks with us," said Horace. "You hardly have time to get the baking done. This is a serious undertaking. My mother used to start as soon as the Thanksgiving turkey came out of the oven." He winked at the girls. "Since we didn't have a Thanksgiving turkey, I think an extra special Christmas dinner is in order. I'll be sure to get the ingredients for my favorite cookies."

Merry spoke up, "You should leave now, Mother, so we can get ready . . . ."

Iris clamped a hand over Merry's mouth. "Shh! You'll ruin everything," she complained.

The morning sun reflected on the snow. The thermometer outside the kitchen window read ten below zero. Iris called to her mother, "Stay warm!"

"Impossible," her mother hollered back.

The girls waved from the kitchen window as the Oldsmobile crunched down the icy drive to the plowed road.

As soon as the car was out of sight, Laughing Sky spoke up, "We don't have much time. My brother will be here before lunch with the tree."

Iris set to work popping corn. Merry settled by the fireplace with a darning needle and strung fluffy popped corn on thread. Laughing Sky carried boxes down from the attic. "Decorations" was written on them in a spidery scrawl.

Martha Rose called her sisters into the kitchen, and they stood around the table as the young Ojibway woman cut the string on the first box and pulled out a wooden shed. "Ah!" she said, "I think we have discovered the nativity scene. Iris, see what's in here."

Iris unwrapped white muslin from a carved figure. "Oh, a shepherd! Isn't he beautiful!" She turned the dark wooden figure in her hands. It was a young man with a shepherd's crook and a lamb over his shoulder. His tunic looked like the carved folds would shift in a breeze.

Laughing Sky handed a lumpy shape to Merry. "An angel," Merry said. "Look at her wings. She looks like she just flew in here."

"There's not enough kings," said Martha Rose.

"We've just started unwrapping," said Merry.

"I know," said Martha Rose with a pout.

Sure enough, when the box was empty, the table held an angel, two shepherds, three sheep, a donkey, the holy family and two kings.

A loud knock on the back door broke the quiet spell. When Iris opened the door, an enormous Christmas tree danced into the room.

Merry clapped her hands, and Martha Rose squealed with

Carol Pearce Bjorlie

delight. Over the noise, Laughing Sky called out, "Take it straight through to the living room."

A tall broad-shouldered man propelled the tree through the room. He was an Ojibway and wore soft leather boots.

"This is One Deer, my quiet brother," explained Laughing Sky. One Deer returned to the kitchen, and his sister introduced him to each of the girls.

He smiled and nodded his head to each of them. "Let's get started," he suggested.

Iris found ornaments made from straw: stars, tiny baskets, donkeys and birds. There were balls of papier-mâché and crocheted snowflakes stiffened with starch. There were also carved horses painted blue or red with white daisies on them. The boxes held fat wooden candle holders and a Christmas cloth that Iris knew would fit the table perfectly.

When the tree was finished, Iris and Merry smoothed a white sheet under the branches and placed the nativity scene there. Iris arranged the figures until she was satisfied they were just right. Laughing Sky hung an evergreen wreath on the front door, and Merry placed small branches of cedar on the mantle.

Laughing Sky brought lunch into the room, and they made a semicircle on the floor around the tree. Laughing Sky had made potato pancakes, sausage and, as usual, there was applesauce.

Merry asked One Deer, "Why haven't we seen you?"

"I live on a reservation up north and have come to visit my little sister for Christmas. I will move here in the spring for a short time. Sister is too young to be alone."

Iris thought a while and asked, "Laughing Sky, why don't you live on the reservation?"

"It's a long story, Iris," her friend answered. "I'll make it short. My cabin was a gift to my grandmother, Wise-Eyes, from a grateful family. Wise Eyes was asked to come and help a family near here who were recovering from measles and whooping cough. The mother got pneumonia. The doctor in town knew of the tribal healing women and went up and

40

fetched my grandmother to assist the family and get them back on their feet.

"She lived in a lean-to near the house. She stayed almost a year, partly because she was needed and partly because of the friendship that built up over time. The farmer and his wife built a cabin for her. It's always been here, mostly empty. I used to love to visit my grandmother when I was a girl. It was a long way from the reservation. My grandmother used to help the town's doctors when folks were recuperating from illness. I come here sometimes to be near town where I sell blankets and scarves I weave. I also help out when Dr. Brenna needs me. We learn from each other."

"So the cabin was a thank you gift?" asked Iris.

"Yes, for saving four lives," answered Laughing Sky.

*****

After lunch, Merry fell asleep on the sofa, and Martha Rose made a pallet for her dolls under the tree. She lay down beside them and soon she too was asleep.

One Deer swept pine needles from the kitchen floor. Iris came in to help Laughing Sky take the empty boxes back to the attic.

Iris handed boxes up the steep attic stairs to Laughing Sky.

"May I ask you a question?" Iris said as they were almost finished.

"Yes, anything," she said.

"Did you believe in Santa Claus on the reservation when you were little? Do you believe in him now and why or why not?" she asked.

Her friend answered, "Iris, I believed in magic as a child. It might be reindeer who could fly, enchanted trees, talking birds, turtles who could sing. I still believe in miracles and things I don't understand. Do you believe in Santa Claus?"

Iris answered, "Well, not really. I do know who eats the cookies we leave on the mantel, and it is *not* Santa. I just wish I could be certain . . . . There's something I want real bad."

Carol Pearce Bjorlie

Laughing Sky stopped her work and sat on the top attic step. "What is it? Maybe it's in the trunk of your family's car right now."

"It's not a present. It's a wish."

"Well?" asked Laughing Sky.

"I wish I could be thirteen forever and never leave the farm," she blurted out. "Then the next minute I can't believe I won't go back to Virginia. Mother's homesick. Every time I say something, people laugh. I can't say anything right. I can even hear myself sounding funny. I love this farm. Don't you see? If I could stay thirteen . . . ."

After Iris' outburst, Laughing Sky sat quietly, then said, "I wish I could see your future, but I can't. Do you really want to be thirteen forever? Let's go downstairs. I heard a car."

As soon as Iris' mother came in the kitchen door, she stopped and sniffed the air. "I smell Christmas," she said and walked straight into the living room. Merry and Martha Rose woke up and saw her in the doorway, her mouth open, her eyes shining.

"How did you do this?" she exclaimed.

Iris spoke up, "One Deer helped us. He's Laughing Sky's brother."

Her mother was merrier than Iris had seen her since they arrived in Harmony. Her eyes twinkled, her cheeks were rosy and she had a real grin on her face when she saw the tree. Laura Ellen announced, "We are going to have Christmas at the Andersens. Not a blizzard or scarlet fever can stop this family."

Horace knelt in front of the nativity scene. "I bet I haven't seen this in twenty years," he said.

"Who made it?" asked Iris.

"My uncle Harald. He used the faces of people he knew. The shepherd has the face of my cousin Leo, and Joseph was modeled after my father. This angel is Aunt Ruth. Isn't she beautiful? People always did say Ruth was the prettiest girl in Fillmore County. The kings are Sigurd and Ignatius, uncles of mine, but Uncle Harald never made the third king. Just didn't get to it."

"Who is dat baby Jesus?" asked Martha Rose.

"I am the baby Jesus," her father answered. "I was an infant when Uncle Harald came for Thanksgiving. A year later he gave this nativity scene to my parents."

"This is a real treasure, Mr. Andersen," One Deer said.

Horace stood up and put an arm around Iris and announced, "Next year we'll have a family celebration for Thanksgiving. We'll invite your uncle Luke. We'll all be healthy, and this table will groan with a turkey so big we'll hardly be able to get it in the oven. It's time the Andersen family celebrated Thanksgiving on the farm again."

"It is?" asked Laura Ellen bleakly.

"It is!" replied Iris.

*****

Two days before Christmas, the Andersen kitchen was coated with a fine layer of flour. Iris and her sisters helped their mother bake the final batch of krumkake cookies for the day. Iris' father had requested almond cookies, so he was at the kitchen table eating leftover nuts.

Martha Rose turned the handle on the flour sifter and was dusted like a sugar cookie. Iris and her mother were using a krumkake iron for the first time. They had learned how hot the iron had to be and how thin the batter of eggs, butter, flour and sugar needed to be to turn out a perfect golden circle. Iris' mother tried to curl the hot discs around the handle of a wooden spoon, the way it was described in the cookbook, but so far there were more misshapen lumps than golden curled cookies.

There was a knock at the door, and when Horace opened it, Pastor Nilsen and Mrs. Nilsen stepped inside. Pastor Nilsen carried a large basket covered with a towel.

Mrs. Nilsen sniffed the air and said, "Umm, what a lovely fragrance! You look like Santa's elves, busy to the last minute."

"Oh, I'm so glad you came," said Laura Ellen from the

43

stove. "Iris and I need some advice on this krumkake thing-a-ma-jig. Let us in on the secret, please." As she spoke, a golden yellow cookie slipped from the fork to the floor.

Mrs. Nilsen unwrapped her scarf and hung her coat on the rack by the door. "All it takes is years of practice," she answered. She came to the stove and turned the heavy krumkake iron on its pivot. She held up a circle of cookie with a fork and wrapped it around the wooden spoon handle, using the fork as a guide.

"Would you look at that!" said Iris. She thought Mrs. Nilsen looked like a Norwegian doll. Her fine blonde hair was the color of sunshine. Today her cheeks were bright from the cold, and her eyes were the color of an autumn sky.

Pastor handed the basket to Horace. Merry and Martha Rose stood nearby, trying to peek at the contents. "Horace, I've noticed something missing from your farm," began Pastor Nilsen in a serious voice like his sermon voice. "When our black Labrador Bess had twelve puppies six weeks ago, we ran out of relatives and friends. Now I've turned to my congregation, hoping they can't refuse. By spring this puppy will be ready to run and rule this farm. She'll also keep these young ladies company." He uncovered the basket, and a friendly black face peered out.

"Is she ours?" asked Merry.

"If your parents agree," he replied as he lifted the fat puppy out of the basket and placed it in Merry's arms. The little animal gave Merry's chin a sloppy swipe with its pink tongue.

"What's her name?" asked Martha Rose.

Pastor Nilsen said, "Don't go too fast. This is with your mother and father's approval."

"Oh, Daddy," began Merry.

Her father stopped her with his raised hand. "I can't think of a better gift. The puppy is ours."

"But, Daddy, what's her name?" repeated Martha Rose.

Mrs. Nilsen answered from the stove, "We call them Pup. You can choose any name that suits you."

Merry called out, "Blackie!"

"That's too easy," replied Iris. "How about Holly, since its Christmas?"

"I like Blackie and she doesn't look like Holly to me," complained Merry.

Laura Ellen suggested, "What about Star?" Both older girls made faces.

"I know! I know!" called out Martha Rose. "Cookie! 'cause we're making cookies."

"Cookie is perfect," said Iris.

The puppy heaved a shuddering sigh and fell asleep in Merry's lap.

Pastor Nilsen turned to Horace. "We have one more doggie delivery to make today, to Earl Runs Like Fox and his boy. They need all the cheer they can get at this time of year."

Iris stood next to Mrs. Nilsen who was still curling krumkake cookies over the wooden spoon. Iris asked her, "Why does Oscar need cheering up?"

Mrs. Nilsen's smile faded, and she answered, "Oh . . . this is Oscar's second Christmas without his mother. She died two years ago on Christmas Eve. She was a beautiful Swedish woman with eyes the color of a lake, like Oscar's. All the ladies at church try to help, but we can't take the place of Ava."

"That was her name, Ava," said Iris. "It's beautiful."

"Like she was," replied Mrs. Nilsen.

Horace pulled out a kitchen chair and said, "Sit down, Pastor. Maybe we can get a cup of coffee and some cookie rejects."

Merry sat motionless with the puppy curled in her lap. Martha Rose's sifter resumed its quick swishing.

Merry breathed deeply and closed her eyes.

"I believe Merry has dozed off," said Mrs. Nilsen.

Merry blinked and said, "Oh, no, I was just . . . saving this time so I won't forget it."

The pastor sat next to her and put his hand on the back of her head, "Merry, my wife and I call this ordinary time when we do an ordinary thing that suddenly makes life special." He stopped. "I believe that the Holy Spirit chooses ordinary times to make us aware of the extraordinary in our everyday life. You'll be back in school in no time."

Merry answered, "I'm going back after Christmas. Dr. Brenna says I can. I'm going to ride the school bus with Iris and everything."

Laura Ellen came to the table with a coffee pot. "Time to try out my first attempt at Scandinavian baking," she announced.

Iris handed around a wooden tray of almond cookies, salted peanut cookies and krumkake.

Martha Rose took a break from her sifter and wiped her floury hands on her sweaty face. "Christmas sure is a lot a work!" she declared.

*****

Laughing Sky and One Deer joined the Andersens for their Norwegian Christmas Eve dinner. Iris had never seen Laughing Sky so beautiful. She wore a dark blue skirt with a wide leather belt and a blouse embroidered with geometric designs. Her braids were arranged in a circle on top of her head.

Martha Rose asked One Deer, "How do she keep 'em up dere?"

One Deer winked at her and said, "Magic!"

Everyone stood in a circle around the table and held hands for the blessing. Iris and the girls decided to share their favorite grace, and she began, "Thank you for the world so sweet,. . . ."

Merry continued, "Thank you for the food we eat."

Martha Rose added, "Thank you for the birds that sing," and all ended together, "Thank you, God, for everything. Amen!"

Their father exclaimed, "Look at all this food! Amen, indeed."

For one brief second Iris thought of Oscar and his father. Were they sitting down to eat? Who cooked?

Iris' mother had used every bowl they owned. There were bowls of mashed potatoes, baked sweet potatoes, Swedish meatballs, pickled herring, canned snap beans, butter, sugar and flat bread. A desert of rumagrut (cream pudding) cooled in the kitchen. Laughing Sky brought a bowl of wild rice cooked with nuts and raisins. A tray loaded with cookies sat on the buffet.

After dinner, Iris and her sisters gave Laughing Sky a necklace of wooden beads they had painted and strung and to One Deer a picture book with drawings by all three girls. He took the book and sat right down on the floor with them and looked at every page, pointing out what he liked best. He hugged the girls and said, "I will always keep this book. When I travel, it will go with me because it carries the spirit of my little sisters."

*****

On Christmas morning the girls stood at the top of the stairs and waited for their father to call them down to open presents. Cookie stood at the bottom of the stairs, panting in excitement. She had slept by the stove on a warm folded blanket all night.

Martha Rose told her sisters, "I heard dat Sandy Claus on my ruf last night."

"Oh, Martha Rose," replied Iris, "You were asleep before you got in bed. One Deer carried you up."

"I heeard him anyway and his deers too," hissed the little girl.

"All ready," called their father.

*****

This was Iris' favorite Christmas moment: before the gifts were opened when the lights on the tree were the only illumination in the room. Her parents stood side by side. Iris wanted to stop and hurry up at the same time.

Under the tree there were three long boxes, one for each girl. Iris opened hers first. There was a Shirley Temple doll with curly hair and a plaid tam. Merry's box held a doll with

47

yellow hair in a blue and white checked dress with a starched white apron of lace. Martha Roses' held a soft cuddly baby doll with a pink blanket.

Santa had put oranges in the toes of each girl's stocking, and there was hard candy too. Iris' stocking had a bottle of Watkins' Lemon Rinse in it. Then Horace placed a small package on Laura Ellen's lap.

Martha Rose had drawn a picture of the farmhouse with Joshua standing in the front yard under a stick tree. She handed it to her father. "Daddy, I made this for you."

He studied the drawing for a long time. "I wish your grandmother could see this. You did a great job, Sweetheart."

Iris had spent a day with thread and a needle sewing a potholder for her mother. She'd used fabric scraps she found it the attic. The potholder was five layers thick, and it had been a real job to get the pieces in line.

Merry gave her parents a piece of paper with a Christmas tree colored at the top and these words underneath: *Merry Christmas, Mother and Daddy. I will not get sick all year long and I love you. Merry Christmas.*

The girls gathered close as their mother unwrapped a leather box with a hinge and clasp of gold. She opened it and took out a gold chain with three oblong pearls dangling from it. "Horace, how in the world . . ."

"They're not from me," he said. "Read the tag."

She read, *For Laura Ellen, a pearl of a girl, from Santa with love.*

"Put them on, Mama," said Martha Rose.

The girls stood by as their mother clasped the gold chain around her neck.

"Oh, dey make your eyes shiny,' said Martha Rose.

Iris' mother leaned over to her husband and kissed him. "If you happen to see Santa, please tell him for me that I love him very much," she said.

"What did Daddy get?" asked Merry.

Laura Ellen handed her husband a flat package wrapped in

paper with Christmas trees on it. He opened the package and took out a book. It had a soft brown leather cover and the blank pages were edged with gold. Over his shoulder Iris read her mother's handwriting on the front page: *Dear Horace, this is a book of empty pages for you to fill with your thoughts, plans and dreams. Love, Santa.*

Martha Rose cried out, "Somebody forgot the story."

Her daddy hugged her. "Oh, there'll be a story!"

Chapter Six

JANUARY

Iris liked to get the mail. Today as she stomped through the blowing snow, she wondered if there would be a letter from Dorothy or Grandmother. When Iris first moved to Minnesota, letters arrived several times a week. Now only Dorothy wrote and her letters came further and further apart.

Iris often lay awake in her bed at night trying to imagine her class. She thought of her best friend. She and Dorothy could talk all night and never run out of things to say. Iris loved spending the night with her. Dorothy's room was the only upstairs room in her house, and they used to lie in bed and giggle half the night. Dorothy had a pink nightgown with lace at the neckline. Iris' new friend from school, Julie, had spent the night once. She wore a red flannel nightgown.

The best letters came from Iris' grandmother. Her father read them aloud. Her mother's hands would lie still in her lap as she listened. A letter from Grandmother was a visit. Her notes chatted about their old neighbor Ted, who had broken his leg at the playground, or tales about Laura Ellen's girlhood or what she and Iris' grandfather had eaten at the most recent church dinner: fried chicken, macaroni and cheese, green beans, jello salad and Rocky Mountain cake for desert. Grandmother ended her letters, *Be safe and happy and remember, I love you all.*

When Iris held a letter from her grandmother, she saw the gentle face before her, smile-wrinkles around her coffee brown eyes, her gray-white hair tucked into a bun at the back of her head. Iris held each letter to her nose and smelled their sweet scent. Grandpa would add a little note and draw a silly picture. She kept every letter in a wooden box under her bed. Dorothy's letters were there, too.

Occasionally her grandmother called. The phone would ring their family's personal code—one short, then one long ring—and the soft voice would crackle over the miles from Richmond to Harmony. Iris' mother always took these calls. As soon as she hung up, the girls crowded around, "What did she say? How's Grandpa?" Iris loved the letters best.

On January twelfth Iris saw the red flag on the mailbox was down and told her mother she was going for the mail. She walked down the snowy driveway path with anticipation.

Iris reached into the box. Two letters! *Both* from Grandmother. The handwriting was unmistakable. She held the letters in her mittens and hurried through the snow. As soon as she opened the kitchen door, she shouted, "Mother! Two letters from Grandma! Two!"

Her mother dried her hands on her apron and said, "Get your Father and Martha Rose; they're in the cellar, sorting seed potatoes."

Merry came in from the living room where she had begun a new puzzle.

When the family was together, Laura Ellen handed the two letters to Horace. He turned them over in his hands, carefully examining the dates. "I don't understand," he said. "These two letters were mailed a week apart but have arrived on the same day. The second letter is addressed to you, "'Laura Ellen,'" not the usual 'Andersen family.'" Iris' father frowned. "I'll read them in the order they were mailed." He slit open the envelope with his pocket knife, pulled out a single sheet of paper and read:

Dear Family,

This letter will be short. Forgive me for not writing sooner, but I've hardly had a minute. Grandpa has pneumonia and I've been nurse. I wanted to call, but he says not to worry you. He is over the worst of it and has begun to eat again and cough less. The doctor says he is on the mend.

51

Carol Pearce Bjorlie

It has been bitterly cold in Virginia. I know you have cold weather, but for us this has been a hardship. Grandpa got sick after working outdoors in the rain. He had been replacing a fence at the back of the yard, and I could not get him to come in. You know how he is when he starts a project.
Be safe and happy and remember, I love you all,
Grandma Pearce

All five of the Andersens sat in silence.

Horace looked up at his wife as he handed her the second letter. "I think you should read this."

"No. We'll hear it together," she said.

Martha Rose spoke up in a trembling voice, "Don't you read it!"

Horace looked at her, sighed and began:

My Dear Daughter,
to write you today is a hard task.

Iris' mother reached for her husband's hand. The house was so quiet that they could hear the clock ticking in her parent's bedroom.

Your father passed away in his sleep yesterday. Uncle Elmo has tried to call Harmony several times, but I guess the weather was bad, and he could never make a connection. Now, Laura Ellen, don't you think about coming home. Your girls need you, and I'm getting along all right. You know, your brother Paul is here, and he'll take care of me. Remember, you were the delight of your father's life.
I love you,
Mother

Horace folded the letter, knelt before his wife and took her in his arms. Iris led her two sisters out of the kitchen and up the stairs. The three of them sat on Iris' bed in silence. She would

52

never forget this day as long as she lived.

Merry broke the silence, "I will never see Grandpa again."

Martha Rose said, "I told Daddy not to read dat letter."

"Oh," sobbed Iris, "I will never get the mail again." Tears began to slide down her cheeks.

Martha Rose pulled back the quilt and covers, "Let's cry," she said.

Soon the three girls were under the covers, holding each other while their tears soaked the pillow.

*****

Laura Ellen called Richmond. Sometimes the telephone line was busy; other times, no one answered. Iris' grandparents lived in a gray frame house four blocks from her old address. Iris could almost see the black telephone on the hall table, could imagine it ringing, ringing in the empty house. Where could her grandmother be?

Iris' mother paced through the house like she was walking in her sleep. She never cried in front of the girls, but Iris knew from her pale skin and red eyes that her mother's life would never be the same. Pastor Nilsen came to visit, and Mrs. Nilsen organized the Lutheran Ladies to bring meals to the house. Laughing Sky spent hours with Laura Ellen, knitting and helping get dinner ready. When things went wrong in Harmony, people cooked.

*****

One afternoon when her mother and father were in the barn, the phone rang its shrill brring, brring. Cookie looked up from the rope she was chewing on the kitchen floor. Iris picked up the receiver and held it to her ear. Then the sweet sound of her grandmother's voice flowed into her ear, "Hello? Hello?"

Finally Iris managed, "Grandma?"

"Iris, is that you? It's so good to hear your voice."

"Grandma, are you all right? Mother and Daddy are in the barn. I'll send Merry out to get them." Iris turned from the

53

phone, "Merry! Grandma's on the phone. Get mother now. Hurry!"

Merry banged out the kitchen door and ran.

"Iris, how is your mother?" asked her grandmother.

"Oh, she's terribly sad, Grandmother. All of us are." Iris swallowed to open her tight throat.

Cookie flopped down across her feet.

"Grandma, Mother ought to be with you." She wondered why no one had brought this up.

"Oh, she couldn't possibly come all this way," began her grandmother, but Iris interrupted.

"Well, why not?"

Laura Ellen hurried into the kitchen and grabbed the phone from Iris. "Mother? Mother! Is that finally you? I've tried and tried to call. I'm so glad to hear you. I want to come home right away." Iris' mother covered her eyes with trembling hands and began to weep as her father entered the back door. He came to his wife and gently took the phone from her and said, "Hello, is this my favorite mother-in-law?"

Iris stood next to her mother and put her arm around her waist and whispered, "Mother, you should go to Richmond and be with Grandma."

"I'd never do it. I've never been away from your father. Think of the money!"

Horace handed his wife his handkerchief, and she wiped her eyes and blew her nose. When he hung up, he turned to her. "Your mother is sending a check to cover the train ticket. I want you to be with her."

Laura Ellen looked from her husband to her oldest child. "I can't leave my family! I can't. Maybe this spring. I'll go this spring. I will."

Iris shook her head, swinging her pony tail from side to side, and blurted out, "I can't believe you, Mother! You think we can't survive without you. Well! If I were you, I'd be gone already. As soon as we got that letter, I wondered, *why isn't she packing*? We aren't babies."

Iris' mother burst into tears and bustled from the room.

Her father watched his wife leave, then stood in front of Iris. He put one hand on her shoulder and said, "Iris, I wish you'd try to think first and then speak. Your mother needs understanding, not judgment. Leaving Virginia and her family has been the hardest thing she has ever done. . . I'm not sure we'll stay." He paused. "A little understanding and a lot of patience will go a long way."

Iris squeezed her eyes shut. She made her grandpa's image come into focus. He looked worried, his brow bumping up into furrows. Grandpa would want her mother to be there. How was it that she knew the right thing to do, and no one would do it? She picked up Cookie and ran upstairs to her room.

*****

Iris and Merry hurried down the school bus steps, raced down the drive and flung open the back door. Their breath came out in puffy clouds and turned to frost on their scarves. Iris headed straight for the warm stove. She pulled her mittens off with her teeth and put her hands on the side of the oven. Cookie looked up from her basket, stood up, stretched and came over to her, wagging her black tail.

"Mother! This is the coldest day of the year, and Mrs. Nervig says if it gets any colder, we won't have school! Today I had to put my coat on after lunch. I never thought I'd be glad to go back to school, but the workers can't get it ready quick enough for me. I'm tired of going to school in a church basement. We can hear the fourth grade class next to us! Oscar's class meets in the big church part, and he says they don't turn up the heat."

"And we're going to get a 'blizzared,'" added Merry. "Mr. Sandgren, the janitor, says so. He can tell when big storms are coming because he feels it in his hands."

"It is a 'blizzard,' Merry. Sometimes you remind me of Martha Rose," said Iris.

"Too bad we all can't be perfect," Merry shot back.

"Girls!" their mother frowned at them both. "Give us some peace here."

Their father sat with Martha Rose in his lap. Martha Rose was holding a book. Her father's hands were wrapped in dish towels. "Your mother's right. Clam up."

"Daddy, what did you do to your hands?" Merry asked.

"Your mother is trying a remedy Laughing Sky told her about for my cracked skin," he answered.

Laura Ellen said, "This dry cold weather is hard on your father's hands. He won't keep his gloves on. Laughing Sky gave me a lotion to apply. I warmed the towels before I wrapped his hands."

"Feels good," her father said. "Plus, it makes me helpless."

"An' I get to turn pages," said Martha Rose.

Laura Ellen turned to her husband, "Horace, since the weather is turning worse, would you go to check on Laughing Sky?" She told Iris, "We've been hearing on the radio about a storm on its way from Canada. When you've warmed your hands, Iris, would you help me bring in extra wood for the fireplace? This morning Martha Rose and I closed up the cracks in the hen house and put out plenty of corn for the chickens."

Iris looked out the window over the sink. Where there would be a garden in the spring, there were now three feet of snow. "I can't get over how pretty a day can be, all sunny and bright, but cold as the North Pole!"

"This cold is dangerous," said her father. "I'll get over to Laughing Sky's before the snow begins to make sure she has enough wood in for the next few days. Who's coming with me?"

"I am, I am," squealed Martha Rose.

"Not I," said Iris. "Tell her to come over here. She can have my bed and I'll sleep with Merry."

Iris' father put on his heavy wool sweater and his parka, wound a woolen scarf around his head and tucked the ends into his coat. Then Laura Ellen buttoned his coat, buckled his boots and pulled a knitted hat down on his head. She gently tugged his mittens over the homemade bandages on his hands.

"Martha Rose, are you ready?" he asked in a muffled voice.

Iris could only see his eyes. She helped her little sister get ready. Martha Rose looked like a teddy bear. The young child grinned and said, "I got on so many coats I can't bend my arms!"

Sure enough, Martha Rose's arms stuck straight out.

"Go and come back quickly," said Laura Ellen. "Here come clouds."

Iris looked through the kitchen door to the north. Sure enough, thick gray clouds were moving their way.

Her father and Martha Rose set off across the pasture. Laughing Sky's cabin was a half mile away behind a slight rise lined with trees. Iris held Cookie so she wouldn't follow them down the path. "You better stay here, little girl; you may be black and easy to find in the snow, but not in a storm like this." Cookie whined.

Laura Ellen suggested, "Iris, you and Merry spend some time with Joshua. Take Cookie for a romp in the barn too. I'll start hot chocolate."

Iris and Merry pulled the horse blanket over Joshua and buckled it in place. He nuzzled Iris' back and seemed to be glad she had thought of him. Cookie pranced around the horse's feet, barking. Joshua nodded his head up and down to show his annoyance at the little critter. Iris pulled his big head down to her eye level, "We haven't forgotten you. You have plenty of oats and water. Stay warm, good old horse, good old horse." She stroked his neck and forehead.

A half an hour later she and Merry pulled the barn door closed. The day had changed from sunny to gray. The wind was bitter in their faces, so the two of them ran to the house, Merry carrying Cookie in her arms.

"Ummm!" Smells good in here," said Merry, sniffing hot chocolate. "Let's have a fire in the living room, and we can read out loud."

"Uncle Luke's books are in my room," said Iris and ran upstairs to get some.

She returned with a fat blue book under one arm. "Mother, I found a perfect poem for tonight: 'Snowbound.'"

"'Snowbound,' that's us," said her mother. "The clouds get lower and lower and look like they will lie down and smother us."

Cookie stood by the back door and began to bark.

Merry called, "Here comes Daddy, Martha Rose. . . . and Laughing Sky!"

Dusk came and Iris could smell the clean scent of snow. No matter what her father said, she knew she could smell snow.

She grabbed Laughing Sky as she came in the door and gave her a quick hug.

"I'm so glad you came. We're going to have a fire in the living room and after dinner, I'm going to read."

"I'm glad to be here," Laughing Sky said. Iris thought she heard relief in her voice. Her thick black hair hung around her shoulders.

"She took off her braids," explained Martha Rose.

"I was brushing my hair when visitors arrived. I hope this isn't too much of a surprise, Laura Ellen,"

Iris' mother said, "You're family, Laughing Sky. We need you to keep our spirits up, and you know we love your company."

"I was getting cabin fever, so I let Martha Rose talk me into coming," she said.

"We didn't want her to get sick," added Martha Rose in a serious voice.

Iris gave her little sister a blank look.

"You know. . . . cabin fever." Martha Rose explained with a wave of her hands.

Seated by the fireplace that evening, Laughing Sky unwrapped Horace's hands, and Laura Ellen rubbed more salve into the cracks. Horace declared himself healed, but Laughing

Sky wrapped them again.

Iris opened her uncle's big book of American poetry. "Now y'all settle down. Listen to the wind!"

Her family quieted while the North Wind keened and whistled around the corners of the house.

Iris began, "Now, Martha Rose and Merry, this is a long poem. Be patient. It's called 'Snowbound' by John Greenleaf Whittier."

She began to read: *The sun that brief December day, rose cheerless over hills of gray, and darkly circled, gave at noon a sadder light than waning moon. . .*

Iris' mother sat on the sofa with Martha Rose cuddled at her side. Horace stretched out on the hearth rug with Merry and Cookie beside him. Laughing Sky sat in the rocker and knitted. Her needles clicked softy as they brushed against one another. A curl of yarn fell from the needle, a pale tan color with flecks of darker brown in the wool.

Iris had pulled in a dining room chair and perched on the edge of it with the book resting on her legs in her lap. On she read, unaware of Martha Rose's even breathing as she fell asleep or the tiny specks of snow and ice that had begun to drift from the sky.

Finally she handed the book to her father, "Daddy, you finish."

He held the book in his awkward hands. "Merry will turn pages," he declared, then cleared his throat and continued the story: *Within our beds awhile, we heard the wind that round the gables roared, with now and then a ruder shock, which made our very bedsteads rock . .*

And finally for the last verse he stood and stretched his towel-wrapped hands before the fire: *Sit with me by the homestead hearth, and stretch the hands of memory forth, to warm them at the wood-fire's blaze!* and he was done.

"Mother, do you think I could be a poetess?" asked Iris.

Her mother smiled, "I think you mean poet," she said. "Yes, I believe you can be anything you want, Iris."

Carol Pearce Bjorlie

Laughing Sky added, "You've told me about your uncle Luke, the writer. Maybe you could send him a letter and ask him how he got started."

"I will," said Iris. "If I'm going to be a writer, I'll need a lot of paper and a new pen."

Merry said, "I love it when we have company. Iris and I get to sleep together like we did in Virginia."

Iris wondered if her sister knew she missed that too.

*****

Iris woke in the middle of the night. She thought of Joshua in the cold barn. She listened to the wind, wondering what had wakened her. She held her breath and listened. There, there was a sound from downstairs. She slipped out of bed without disturbing Merry and put on her slippers. She went down the steps, avoiding the creaky ones, and peeked into the kitchen. Her mother and father sat at the table with their backs to the door. Laura Ellen's head was on her husband's shoulder, and he patted her hair like he did when Iris or her sisters were hurt or sad and he didn't know what else to do. Her mother's shoulders shook as she wept.

Iris tiptoed back upstairs to Merry's room.

The next time Iris woke she could tell by the dim light that snow was falling. Merry had pulled the quilts to her side and buried her head under them.

Iris got up and wrapped an afghan around her shoulders. She sat in a chair by the bedroom window and looked out. Now the flakes were as big as feathers and fell fast and thick. She couldn't see two feet past the window. She sat and watched the blizzard and thought, *I never dreamed of snow like this. It always changes, like the ocean. Sometimes the flakes are no bigger than salt, and now the whole sky was falling.*

She shivered and decided to dress. The she remembered the night scene she had witnessed in the kitchen. She thought of her mother crying because of the long winter, crying because she was homesick, crying because her father had died. Then

60

she thought of Oscar. How he must miss his mother! Sadness fell on the house like a blanket too heavy to lift.

*****

During the night the heavy ice and snow pulled down electric and phone lines. The white farmhouse returned to kerosene lanterns and candles.

Iris and Laughing Sky sat together after breakfast with a pad of paper and the Shumway Garden Guide. Iris' father had told each girl that they could have a section of the family garden for their own. In Richmond Iris' mother had tended a tiny patch of garden in their back yard. She had grown big red tomatoes and flowers: peonies, zinnias, irises and two yellow rose bushes with huge blossoms that she often cut and put in a crystal vase in the center of their dining room table.

While Laughing Sky and Iris chatted about dianthus, or pinks as Laughing Sky called them, and delphiniums (which Iris liked to say), her mother finished up the breakfast dishes and joined them at the table. She took a clean sheet of paper and drew a rectangle.

"Let's plan this garden right," she suggested. "I'm going to prove that I have a green thumb. I am so hungry for a plate of fresh vegetables that I'm going to plant everything I see in this catalogue. Let's order seeds."

Overjoyed at her mother's enthusiasm, Iris pushed the garden guide across the table to her. "Just save a small square for zinnias and mint for me."

Laura Ellen began to turn pages, "Oh, I want everything!" she sighed.

Iris and her friend laughed out loud as her mother read the descriptions of luscious ripe red strawberries or giant juicy Big Boy tomatoes.

Horace came in from the dining room where he and Merry had set a puzzle up on the big table. "My eyes are going crossed," he said. "Those tiny pieces leave me dumbfounded, but Merry puts one in after another."

Carol Pearce Bjorlie

"Come, Daddy, help us with our garden," said Iris.

Her father leaned over the table, "Laura Ellen, my mother used to sit right here with her seed catalogue, draw plans and dream about spring. If I remember correctly, she didn't take kindly to directions. The kitchen garden was all hers."

He stood up straight and flexed his hands carefully. "Well, my hands are better, thanks to my two nurses. I expect I'll have to get back to work." He left and went to the cellar stairs to stoke the furnace.

Within the large rectangle she'd sketched, Laura Ellen separated three small squares for the girls. "Which one do you want, Iris?" she asked.

"Just a sunny spot. I don't care where," said Iris.

She watched all afternoon as her mother sat hunched over the garden guide.

Occasionally she would get up and peer into the snow towards the spot where the garden would be in the spring. Finally she began to draw, erase and design the garden on paper. Iris took the final version and sat down to study it.

"Goodness," her mother said, "the day has flown! I ought to plan more gardens."

There was a sparkle in her mother's eye. Next she sat with Merry and Martha Rose as they chose plants for their gardens. Martha Rose wanted to grow tadpoles but settled for daisies and spinach.

"Martha Rose, you don't even eat spinach," Iris said.

"I will," she answered.

Laura Ellen shrugged her shoulders, "Well, I eat spinach, so we'll order some seeds."

Merry Columbine chose columbine, of course, and Dutchman's-breeches because of their names.

Laura Ellen called to Horace, who had returned to the puzzle with Merry, "Horace, when will the peonies bloom?"

He stood in the doorway, "I think late May or June. There are tulips and crocus too, but I don't remember where they are. They come up first. You know, Laura Ellen, maybe you should start small the first year."

"Oh no," said his wife, "I've heard you talk about this black soil all my married life, and I am going to have a garden!"

"By all means," said her father, "don't let me dissuade you. Just wear gloves and keep your hands nice," he teased.

Iris asked, "Mother, may I be your helper? You can teach me."

"We'll be learning together, Iris, and yes, I will count on you as assistant gardener." Her mother reached across the table and shook her hand.

Beyond her mother's head, Iris noticed the snow swirling around the corner of the house, settling in a drift taller than she was.

Merry came into the kitchen rubbing her eyes. "I can't look at that puzzle any more today. Let's play hide-and-seek."

Laughing Sky turned to Laura Ellen with a mischievous smile, "Let's join the girls!"

"We'll show them how to hide," Laura Ellen said in agreement.

Iris was so surprised at her mother's response that she urged, "You be first, Mother!"

"Are you really, really, really going to play with us, Mama?" asked Martha Rose.

"I certainly am! Everyone put their heads down, no peeking, and count to fifty—slowly." Laura Ellen was already moving out of the room as she spoke.

Iris had a flashback; she remembered her mother playing hide-and-seek with her when she was small, but for years Merry and Iris had entertained their little sister.

Merry counted in a loud voice, "Forty-eight, forty-nine, fifty! Here we come, ready or not!"

The girls jumped up.

"I bet she's under my bed," said Martha Rose. "That's where I always hide."

"Thanks for telling," said Merry. "She couldn't have gone upstairs without the steps creaking. I listened."

Iris opened the basement door and ran down the steps. There wasn't much space to hide in there. When she came upstairs, Laughing Sky was lifting the long tablecloth and peering underneath the table. "Not here," she called.

Merry searched behind the living room sofa. "Not here," she called out.

Then Iris saw a motion in the long draperies. Her eyes went to the floor. A pair of black shoes stuck out from under the floor-length fabric. She went quickly and found Martha Rose wandering in the kitchen on tiptoe calling, "Where are you, Mama?" Iris took her little sister by the hand, led her to the curtains and pointed at the toes of her mother's shoes.

Martha Rose flung back the curtain and called out, "Dere you are! I found you!"

Then she pointed her finger at her mother. "Don't you ever hide again. I don't like wondering where you was."

"Oh, really?" asked her mother. "Now you know how it feels to be a mother."

Chapter Seven

FEBRUARY

The temperature in Harmony dropped to -30 degrees on the first day of February. Iris was furious. She wrote to Dorothy. *"The weather is just not fair! It snowed and got cold, snowed some more, got colder, coldest, then it got even colder. Thirty degrees below zero. I'm so mad I could spit. There's nothing I can do about it. We've played games, had fires, dressed up Martha Rose, brushed Cookie 'til she doesn't have a stray hair and been out to the barn to feed Joshua and groom him. I wear so many clothes I can hardly move. You would not believe this. You wouldn't! You probably think I'm fibbing. Well, if you could see me now, wrapped in an afghan with two pairs of pajamas on and Mother's wool sweater, you'd believe me. Dorothy, what am I doing here?"*

All three girls missed their friends. Iris and Merry had lost two weeks of school because power lines and phone lines were down and roads impossible. Martha Rose and her father didn't go into town. It kept snowing. Iris' dad shoveled snow up on banks over his head so he could get to the barn.

Laughing Sky spent two nights and then decided to go back to her cabin. Iris and her dad walked over with her and brought stacks of wood up to the porch. First, they had to find the wood, knocking down four feet of snow from the pile. Laughing Sky said she'd use the time to weave. Laura Ellen sent two loaves of bread and a large bowl of soup with them when they left the house.

On the way home Iris noticed the barn door. "Daddy, look! The barn door blew open."

Just then Oscar came out. He ran towards the house, hunkered down, head covered in a heavy scarf and an Indian blanket over his coat, but Iris knew it was Oscar.

Iris' father ran to meet him. "Come in. Be quick!"

The three of them blustered into the kitchen and headed to the fireplace. Cookie, interrupted from her nap, barked and snorted away.

Iris' mother came over. She took one look at Oscar, hugged him, unwound the scarf from his head and smoothed the hair out of his eyes. "Oscar, how on earth did you get here? Are you all right?"

Oscar pulled away, heaving to get his breath. "I wrapped Blue's feet. I had to . . . get here. Dad's gone. Went out . . . didn't come back! He was going to . . . chicken coup. . ."

"Sit down," said Horace. "Get your breath. Laura Ellen, some hot water, or tea—with sugar. Lots of sugar."

Iris could see Oscar trying not to cry and trying to breathe at the same time. No calming him down! Iris didn't blame him.

Oscar continued, "No phone—nobody outside. You aren't the closest but I knew you'd help. People in town . . . sissies. Oh, sorry."

"Don't worry," said Iris' mother. "I've called them worse!"

Oscar almost smiled.

*****

Horace said, "Oscar, warm up here a bit. I'll get the tractor out and try to get to your place."

"Daddy, I'm coming!" Iris interrupted. "I can sit in front of you. I'll help keep you warm. I have to come."

Her father looked at her. "Get your coat on. We might need you at the house."

"Horace, you can't mean that!" his wife said with a frown.

"Yes. I do. You stay here with the little girls."

Iris ran upstairs and began to dress. Her heart thundered. Thirty below zero, and Oscar's father was outside! She put on her mother's big coat, two scarves and gloves under her mittens. She pulled the scarves over her face so that only her eyes showed. Her mother pulled a big wool hat down over her head. "Now the scarves won't blow away." She grabbed Iris hard, "Oh, don't let these men do anything stupid!"

*****

The three of them left the house. Blue was ready to do anything, go anywhere Oscar wanted. The tractor clanked to life and moved as slowly as a turtle down the drive.

It was beyond cold. Iris leaned into her father for warmth and safety. He had let her come with him.

Oscar's house was one block from town. He'd said it was the house his mother grew up in, and Iris had seen it but never been inside. The outbuildings included a small barn for the two horses and a chicken coop behind it. Snow wasn't falling. Dad said it was too cold to snow, but it was blowing around. Drifts against Oscar's house were halfway up the windows. There wasn't much of a path beside the house, but the tractor led the way, and they stopped in front of the barn. Oscar jumped off Blue and hurried the horse inside.

Her father helped her down and jumped off behind her. He grabbed her by her arms. "Iris, I want you to go inside and start a fire in the kitchen fireplace. Warm the place up. Then look for blankets. I am going to find this man, bring him in and get him warm. Make some tea or coffee if you can find it. If anyone comes by, tell them we're out back. Lord, have mercy on us all."

"Daddy . . ." Iris began.

"Go!"

*****

Iris went into Oscar's house through the back door. She could hardly believe two men lived here. It was neat with an empty feeling. There was a small round table with three chairs in front of the fireplace. No rocker. No happy dog on her bed in front of the fire. No sound at all. There were blue gingham curtains at the kitchen windows and one candle on the table. Matches were nearby, so she lit the candle, then saw two kerosene lanterns on the mantle above the stove. She lit them. That was better.

Blankets. She walked into the next room, the front room, and there was a small sofa with an Indian blanket on it. She grabbed it up and another one she saw over a wooden chest. There was a picture on the chest, and she looked at the young woman in it. It was Oscar's mother. She had gold hair in braids that circled her head. Even in black and white, Iris could tell his mother's eyes were blue. Her smile was wide and genuine, a happy woman. She carried the blankets into the kitchen, pulled a chair in front of the fireplace and placed the blankets over it. Wood. She needed wood. There was a small pile next to the fireplace. Oscar had let the fire go out. She placed the wood in the fireplace, found old newspapers nearby and shoved some under the wood. Matches were on top of the fireplace, and she lit the fire, blowing on it and waving the flames to life.

Tea was next. There was a shiny copper kettle on the stove with water in it, and Iris looked in a drawer for tea bags. It felt funny to be in Oscar's house, looking around. There was a white wooden cabinet on one side of the fireplace and a bookcase on the other side. She opened one door of the cabinet, and there were tea bags and coffee. She was set.

When would they come in with Earl? Oscar must be out of his mind with fear.

She was beginning to sweat and realized she had all her outdoor clothes on. She began to peel the layers away.

*****

There was a knock at the front door. She ran to it and opened it. Mr. Hansen, the postman, stood there with mail in his hands. "Iris? What are you doing here?"

"Oh, Mr. Hansen, Earl's lost in the snow . . ."

Before she could finish her sentence, he hurried into the house, put the mail down and asked, "Where's Oscar? Is your father here?"

She pointed to the back door. "Mr. Runs Like Fox went out

Sweet Harmony

to check on the horses and didn't come back. Oscar couldn't find him!" The words came faster and she ran out of breath.

He took her arm. "You look set here. Good."

And he was gone out the back door before she could answer.

Iris looked for a clock. What time was it? How close to dusk could it be? They'd never find Earl if it got dark, and it got dark here around 3:30 in the afternoon, another thing Iris couldn't get used to. She remembered that her family had had lunch, so it *was* afternoon. There, there was a clock on top of the bookcase. It was a beautiful carved wooden clock. She thought of Oscar or his father winding it every morning. It read 2:00. She was relieved.

She looked out the kitchen window towards the barn, but snow was blowing so hard she couldn't make out any figures. Wind was worse than snow. She didn't even see Mr. Hansen's footprints. She began to look at the books. They must have been Oscar's mother's books. She'd been a teacher. There were a lot of poetry books, plays by Shakespeare and Marlowe. Who was that? There were cookbooks and newspapers from St. Paul. How did you get a newspaper from St. Paul in Harmony? She wished she'd known Oscar's mother, Ava. Mrs. Nilsen had said her name was Ava.

She walked into the living room. There were thick sky-blue curtains here. Not much furniture, though, a small red sofa with the chest in front of it. She saw more bookcases, three of them. There was a chair in front of each one, like someone had sat there and looked for a book. The fireplace was cold, and above the mantle there was a painting of the sea.

There was a blast as the back door blew open. Her father carried Earl in his arms. Earl's eyes were closed, his face and hair covered in snow and blood. Oscar was close behind, with Mr. Hansen closing the door behind him. "I'm going across the street to tell Ruth where I am. I'll be back." He ran out the front door.

Oscar looked at Iris with blank eyes. "I couldn't find him

and he was right there! Right there!"

She grabbed his arm. "But you did find him. You did!"

"He hit his head. He must have slipped in the hay loft or on the ladder. I looked but I never saw him." Oscar fell into a chair at the table, put his head in his hands and began to sob.

"Os-car, Os-car," a faint sound, more grind than voice, came from Earl. His whole body trembled. Horace had sat him in the chair in front of the fire, blankets around his shoulders. The teapot began to sing.

Iris jumped up and put a teabag in the teapot and removed it from the fire.

"Tea!" she said. Earl still shivered.

Horace took a kitchen towel, held it close to the fire and then placed it on the side of Earl's head. It came away bloody.

A groan emerged, "Ah, ah." Then Earl stirred, moving his feet back and forth.

"Let's get your shoes off, Earl." Iris' father knelt to untie Earl's boots, removed two pairs of socks and then held each of Earl's feet in his warm hands.

"Ah!" Earl almost yelled.

Oscar sat up, brushed his eyes with his fists and came to his father's side. "I couldn't find you! You didn't come back. You didn't come back." He was sobbing again. Iris could feel his misery inside her.

Iris watched as Earl slowly raised one hand and placed it on Oscar's head. "I'm back," said the gravelly voice.

Horace spoke to Oscar. "Pull a mattress in here, and let's let him lie down. We'll pile blankets on him. Iris, can you find more blankets?"

Oscar spoke with a hiccup, "There, there . . . are more in the chest in the living room."

Iris ran to get them. The front door opened and Mr. Hansen and Dr. Brenna came in. The tiny house seemed full of people.

Dr. Brenna walked into the kitchen just as Oscar and Horace moved Earl onto a mattress in front of the fire.

Dr. Brenna said, "Horace, looks like you've done just what

I would have done. Earl, let me see that scrape. Now how did you do this?"

Horace moved out of the way and Dr. Brenna moved close. "You've got a deep scrape here, Earl. Gonna' give you heck but won't kill you! I'll clean that up and bandage it. Good thing you didn't fall outside. It was cold enough in the barn to get you started on some frostbite, but warm enough to keep you alive!"

Oscar continued to murmur, "I couldn't find him. I couldn't find him. The barn door was open, but I couldn't see him."

Horace put his arm around the young man and said to him, "You did find him. You were the one who saw him behind the ladder. He was in the dark. No one could see him. Oscar, we were just in time."

"Indeed," added Dr. Brenna.

Iris looked at Earl. He had fallen asleep while Dr. Brenna was bandaging his head.

Dr. Brenna stood up. "Let him sleep. When he wakes up, tea, oatmeal and warm bread. Oscar, come get me anytime. I mean it. I'll be back in the morning."

"Yes. Yes, I will come get you."

"Same for me," said Mr. Hansen. "Ruth's bringing soup over in a half hour."

"We'll be fine . . . " began Oscar.

"Yes, you will," began Mr. Hansen, "because we're going to do everything we can to get your father back to good health. He's a tough one; you know that."

"Yes, sir," answered Oscar.

Dusk was falling as Iris and her father left Oscar's house. Mrs. Hansen had brought soup and bread. Earl had drunk three cups of tea and sat up. Oscar had plenty to do. Iris hated the thought of leaving the two of them in that quiet house. "I'll come by tomorrow," said Horace. "I have a feeling you and your dad are going to get a lot of attention, Oscar. You ready for that?"

Oscar mumbled, "We don't need help. Dad's got me."

71

"Well, you're going to have to turn these town folk away."
He looked at Iris with a grin. "Ready for the tractor ride of your
life?"

Chapter Eight

MARCH

Iris leaned over the kitchen sink. When her mother poured Watkins' lemon rinse over her head, Iris' hair was a golden stream. Laura Ellen wrapped a towel around her daughter's head, and Iris stood up, dizzy after being bent over so long. She took the towel from her mother and began to dry her hair.

"Mother, do you think the dogwoods are blooming in Richmond? That's the only tree I know of that we don't have here, and I miss them."

Her mother smiled, "March is early for dogwoods. Please don't forget magnolias or wisteria."

Iris looked at the freezing rain that pelted the ground. "Well, if this was snow, we'd be having a blizzard. If I went out now, I'd be up to my neck in mud!"

Her mother laughed. "Your father can hardly lift his feet sometimes, the mud gets so thick on his boots. 'Remember,' he says, 'this is not the end of snow.'"

Martha Rose came into the kitchen and slumped in a chair. "I don't have nufin' to do."

"Martha Rose, your speech is suffering today," said her mother.

"So am I," replied the little girl. "Where's Merry?"

"She's drawing, reading or napping in her room," responded her mother.

"Then where's Cookie?"

Her Mother sighed, "In the barn with your father."

"I'll play with you while my hair is drying," offered Iris.

"Kin I be boss?" asked her sister.

"Yep. You're the boss. What's next?"

"I want to go up, up, up in the attic and put on dresses," said Martha Rose.

"I'll play for an hour."

She heard her mother sigh, "Thanks be to God."

The Andersens' attic was a jumble of boxes. Iris found some stout wooden cases used to pack linens and blankets when they moved. She pushed them aside. "Look, Martha Rose, we could put these on top of each other and use them as book cases or shelves to keep things on."

"Find the dress-up clothes."

Iris called out, "Here they are." When she was little, she loved to wear old hats with nets and veils. The idea of being a grown-up made dressing in her mother's old Sunday dresses and shoes fun for rainy days. She and Merry passed hours changing outfits and standing in front of a mirror, and after finding the perfect ensemble, parading in front of their parents. While Martha Rose tried on straw hats and flowered summer dresses, Iris continued to poke around in the attic.

"You know, Martha, when we moved in, we jumbled our boxes in front of a lot of stuff. There's no telling what we'll find." Iris noticed a dusty hooded cradle and wondered if her father had slept in it when he was a baby. "Look, a cradle. We can take it downstairs and you can put your dolls in it."

"It's for our brudder," her sister answered. She walked up to Iris with a fur neck piece, "Here, put this fox on me," she demanded, and Iris attached the mouth of the fox fur to its tail with a clamp that opened and closed.

"These things are awful," she exclaimed.

Martha Rose ignored her. "I'm going to show Mama how this fox bites himself."

"Hold onto the hand rail," called Iris. She moved a tall lamp next to a dresser and opened the top drawer. Inside were papers, yellow and crumbling. She continued to open drawers, finding books and more paper. Next she opened a trunk that sat under the attic window. She liked it a lot. There was a place for it in her room. After dusting and furniture wax, it would make a good surface to set things on at the foot of her bed. She lugged the trunk to the top of the steps by the leather strap. *Too heavy*, she thought, and decided to empty it.

She unhooked the metal latches on the front of the chest and opened it. There were books on top, more books! No wonder it was heavy. She lifted them out and placed them in the crates she found. There was a book that had the complete plays of Shakespeare and a yellow leather book called "Plutarch's Lives," and a Bible and hymnal in Norwegian.

Underneath the books was a sheet folded around fabric. She lifted it out and unwrapped the sheet. An ivory silk dress was there, and as Iris held it up, she realized it was a special dress. It had pearls sewn around the neck, and the waist came down in a V. The long sleeves were edged in yellowed lace, and there was a ruffle of lace at the neck. She took off her sweater and skirt and slipped the pale dress over her head. She tried to fasten a row of buttons behind her back and decided she needed help. She lifted the long skirt and carefully descended the stairs.

"Mother," she called. "Mother, look what I found!"

When Iris came into the kitchen, her mother said, "My, how beautiful you look. I would guess that is your Grandmother Andersen's wedding dress."

"Do you think so? It fits me, except it's too long. Would you do up the buttons in back?"

Laura Ellen fastened the long row of tiny cloth-covered buttons, then turned Iris around, tilted her head and closed her eyes. "Go look at yourself in my mirror."

Iris trailed the ivory gown into her mother's room and stood before the long mirror, staring at the image of a young woman who stared back at her. She lifted her long blond hair and pulled it back from her face, wondering, *Has anyone had this dress on since Grandmother's wedding? Will I be like her? Oh, I wish I knew you, Grandmother.*

Iris returned to the kitchen. "I'm going to wear this when I get married," she declared.

Her mother said, "You may change your mind."

"Daddy says that Grandma was eighteen when she got married. I won't change my mind about the dress."

Martha Rose stood nearby in her straw hat and studied her big sister. "You'll never get married. You don't know any boys."

"What are you talking about? I know lots of boys!"

"Only Oscar, and you can't marry him," said Martha Rose.

"Martha Rose, I said I would play with you, but an hour is up, and you have to put those clothes away. You look ridiculous! Why couldn't I marry Oscar if I wanted to?"

"Because he already asked me at the hardware store this week!" Martha Rose stomped up the stairs, her colorful skirt dragging behind her.

Iris and her mother burst into laughter.

"I can never stay angry with her," said Iris. She called after her little sister and said, "I doubt if he'll wait for you to grow up. He is fifteen, you know."

Her mother seemed almost gay and said, "I think you should call the prospective bridegroom and invite him and his father to dinner."

"Who?" asked Iris.

"Oscar," answered her mother. "His dad is well enough to ride again. We'll invite Laughing Sky. Her brother has been gone for six weeks, and everyone must feel as cooped up as we do. I know your father would enjoy the company of another farmer. He and Earl can decide on a day to go to Rochester to buy their seed corn at the co-op."

"Mother, I won't call Oscar, but you may," said Iris.

"All right, I'll call him if you will put on your boots and invite Laughing Sky." Her mother went to the phone.

Through a front window of the log cabin, Iris saw her friend working at her loom and knocked on the window. Laughing Sky came to the door. "Hello, Iris. I need a visitor. This rain feels like it is pounding on my head instead of this tin roof."

Iris listened to the drumming rain overhead and said in a loud voice, "We want you to come to dinner. Mother is inviting Oscar and his father. She says not to bring anything; we'll just have something good—stew, maybe. Will you come?"

"I wouldn't miss it," said Laughing Sky. "If you can wait a minute, I'll finish this row of weaving and walk over with you."

Iris watched Laughing Sky's hands move, picking up strands of yarn and unraveling the threads. She looked like she was playing music, her hands moving rhythmically and gracefully. She said, "I found my wedding dress today in our attic. It was my grandmother's, and I'm going to wear it when I get married. I'm going to get married at eighteen, just like my grandmother."

"Oh, Iris, eighteen is young!" said Laughing Sky as she got up from her work.

"My grandmother didn't think it was young. You should see the dress. I don't even look like myself in it."

"But, Iris, I like the way you look."

"I just want you to know, I'm making plans."

"I thought you were going to be a poet," said Laughing Sky.

"I can write poems and be married," Iris added.

"I guess you'll write love poems."

"When are you going to get married?" asked Iris.

"Oh, I don't plan to marry. I'm twenty-six and marriage would complicate my simple life. I like it the way it is."

When Iris and Laughing Sky arrived at the house, Laura Ellen announced that, sure enough, Oscar and his father were going to come for dinner. "Oscar says he'll be glad to get a decent meal."

Laughing Sky said, "Put us to work. What can we do?"

Laura Ellen thought for a moment, "First let's put the leaf in the table. We'll have eight for dinner. Then, Iris, you can find the yellow tablecloth so it will look cheery and set the table. Call Merry. She loves to turn sausages on the big frying pan. Your father is in the barn monkeying with the tractor. I'm sure the men will head out there as soon as they finish their last bite. That tractor is going to be so well-oiled it will slide out of the barn this spring."

As Iris and Laughing Sky set the table, Iris said, "As soon as dinner is done, I'll put the wedding dress on for you."

"I can hardly wait," said Laughing Sky.

Soon they heard the sound of hooves sloshing up the muddy drive. "Oscar and his daddy are here," shouted Martha Rose as she hurried down the steps.

Oscar's father was a small quiet man. The few times Iris had seen him, he rarely spoke to her, only touched his forehead and nodded. When Earl took off his hat, he still had a bandage on his scalp wound.

As soon as Oscar saw Martha Rose, he held out his arms and she jumped into them and almost sent him sprawling.

"Martha Rose!" said Laura Ellen. "You almost knocked Oscar down. Say hello to Mr. Runs Like Fox, Oscar's father."

Oscar set Martha Rose down and she held out her little hand, "Hello, Mr. Fox. What did you do to your head?" she said in her sweetest voice.

To Iris' surprise, when Oscar's father took his hand out of his pocket, it had a small harmonica in it. "Goodness," he said, "how did that get there?" He put the musical instrument to his mouth and played a melody: *You are my sunshine, my only sunshine . . .*

Oscar smiled at Martha Rose's open mouth, "That's my Dad's way of saying, 'Hello.'"

"Can I do dat?" asked the little girl.

Oscar's father kneeled in front of Martha Rose and said, "I will teach you."

Before anyone could say "Hello" or "Could I take your hat?" Martha Rose took Oscar's father by the hand and led him into the living room.

"Come with me," she said.

Iris' mother said, "Oscar, would you go out to the barn and

drag my husband away from that machinery? Make sure your horses are at home in the barn with Joshua."

During dinner Martha sat next to Earl Runs Like Fox. Iris sat across the table from him. When he took his hat off, his hair amazed her. It fell thick and black to his shoulders. He had a habit of tucking it behind his ears. Dr. Brenna had cut off a long hank of it above his left ear where his bandage covered his wound.

Iris' father kept a conversation going about crops, red Pontiac potatoes and DeKalb corn. Earl rarely spoke and kept his eyes lowered. Finally he put his napkin beside his plate, took a deep breath and said, "Mrs. Andersen, such a meal!" He put his hand on the yellow tablecloth. "A woman's touch is nice."

"I know you and Horace have a trip to Rochester planned and should fire up that tractor. Go on out to the barn. I'll enlist Oscar and Iris to help. We'll be done in a jiffy," she said.

Iris complained, "Mother, I want to put on the wedding dress and show Laughing Sky."

"Wedding dress?" said Oscar.

"Iris is gettin' married," Martha Rose confided to Earl Runs Like Fox.

Her father moved back from the table, "On that note, Earl, I think we should retire to the barn."

"Will you come back and play dat 'monica, please?" pleaded Martha Rose.

Oscar's father answered, "I'll play you to sleep."

Iris and Oscar passed one another as they cleared the table, bringing dishes and glasses to the kitchen. When the tablecloth was removed and the leaf put away, she asked, "Mother, may I go upstairs and put on the dress?"

Her mother smiled, "Go on, Beautiful. We'll call your father. He'll want to see this."

Iris hurried up the stairs. She took the dress off the bed where she had placed it and lifted it once more over her head. Besides the musty smell, there was a faint fragrance. Perhaps it was her grandmother's perfume, the one she had worn on her wedding day.

Iris stood with her eyes closed. Her father had a few pictures of his parents, and her grandmother had worn her hair in braids that formed a crown on the top of her head. Iris took her own long braid out and began to plait two braids, winding them in a circle on her head, securing them with hair pins.

Then she went down the stairs. Everyone was at the kitchen table. She could hear Merry telling Martha Rose to put the forks and knives away. Merry hated to sort things and gave these jobs to her little sister. Iris slipped quietly into her mother's bedroom to look at herself in the dress again. If she turned her back to the mirror, she could just about fasten all the buttons on the back of the dress by looking over her shoulder. There, she was done. She smoothed out the front of the dress with her hands.

As Iris entered the kitchen, the back door opened. Cookie pranced in, followed by her father and Earl. Suddenly the notes of "Beautiful Dreamer" floated in the air. Oscar's father had the harmonica in his mouth, and his eyes were closed as he played. Her father came close and examined the dress, and Laura Ellen leaned against the sink as the song came to a close. Laughing Sky looked first at Iris, then at Oscar, whose mouth gaped open.

Martha Rose spoke in the silence, "See, Iris is gettin' married and she ain't even old enough."

Chapter Nine

APRIL

Iris sat on the back steps watching cloud formations. Today they looked like her father's handkerchiefs hanging on the line, long wisps of them. Her father liked to say, "When spring comes, Minnesota has a party." Lilac bushes were covered with tender green leaves and tight fists of promising blossoms. Tulips, soon to be pink as a kitten's tongue, poked up in a line next to the drive, and narcissus and daffodils were making promises in a bed beside the front door. Iris and her mother had cleared the garden patch with hoes and a rake. Horace said it was still too early to plant. "Could still snow . . . "

She heard a creak and saw the barn door open. Martha Rose poked her head out and looked left, then right. She spotted Iris on the steps and put her finger to her lips. What was she up to? Her little sister came cautiously out of the barn, dragging her father's big wood-splitting ax behind her in the dirt. It left a deep groove as it trailed behind her.

Iris sprang up. "Martha Rose! You put that ax right back where you found it. Daddy would have a fit if he saw you dragging his good ax in the dirt."

"Sit down, Iris," Martha said with a pout. "I am gonna' kill that wooster!" She plopped down on the step Iris had vacated and leaned the ax against her knees.

Iris grabbed the ax, "I'm going to take this right back to the barn. You could cut your foot off!"

Martha Rose squealed, "I am gonna' ax his head off!"

Iris looked at the fury on her sister's face. "Martha Rose, the reason Sam chases you is that you run from him. Wave your hands, stand your ground and he won't bother you. Don't let him boss you around. He's only a rooster."

Carol Pearce Bjorlie

Martha Rose scrabbled the dirt with the toe of her shoe as she watched her sister carry the ax to the barn. "Come back, Iris," she called. "Here he comes! Bring the ax, bring the ax!"

Iris stood at the barn door, "Martha, here's your chance. When he gets close, stamp your feet and holler, 'Git, Sam, git!'"

The dazzling rooster approached Martha Rose. She picked up a dirt clod and tossed it at the bird. "Shoo. Shoo, Sam. Go 'way!" she hollered.

The bird stalked steadily towards the little girl, his head shifting forward with each step, as his scrawny yellow legs picked their way across the yard. Martha Rose yelled at Iris, "He's not going away. He's gonna' bite me!"

"No, he's not," insisted Iris. "Stay put. You surprised him." She watched as the bird picked up speed and hurtled towards her sister. Then she shouted, "Run!"

Martha Rose leaned down and picked up another dirt clod, threw it and missed. The bird flapped his wings. Martha Rose found a rock. As she bent over, the angry bird squawked and jumped on her. Martha Rose fell backwards.

Iris gripped a shovel that leaned next to the barn door and ran into the yard.

She whacked Sam with the back of it and with a thunk sent him flying. She sat down on the ground next to her sister, who lay screaming. Her mother ran out of the kitchen door.

Martha Rose held her face. Blood trickled between her fingers.

Laura Ellen picked up her youngest and carried her into the house. Iris followed. Her mother set Martha Rose on the kitchen table. In a calm voice, she said, "Martha Rose, honey, move your hands and let me see what that darn rooster's done."

Martha Rose continued to shriek, but pulled her hands away from her face. She kept her eyes screwed tight. Iris said, "Sam's gone, Martha Rose. You can open your eyes."

Terrified, her little sister continued to cry, "He bit me. He bit me. I told you. You didn't listen. Now I'm bleeded."

Iris felt like crying when she saw the nasty wound on her sister's face. A deep triangle of flesh had been torn away. Her mother looked it over and said, "I think we need to have Dr. Brenna look at this. Iris, get your daddy. Tell him we need to head to the doctor's. You and Merry stay here. She's up in her room drawing."

Her mother turned to Martha Rose and said, "Let's clean you up a bit. Iris, get a wet towel from the kitchen." When Iris returned, her mother began to mop at Martha's bloody clothes and neck as Iris headed out to the near field where her father and Earl Runs Like Fox were sowing wheat. She could hear her sister's screams all the way.

Iris found her father and the two of them hurried to the house. As she went past the body of the rooster, she knew she should deal with the bird. Her mother came out of the house carrying Martha Rose in her arms. Iris asked, "Mother, what should I do with Sam?"

Her sister yelled out, "Kick him!"

Her mother raised an eyebrow and said, "Bury him behind the barn."

"Can't I come with you?" asked Iris.

"Not this time. Stay with Merry. Dr. Brenna will clean and bandage this properly. Get rid of that bird so we will never have to see him again, and I will be a happy woman."

Iris watched as her father drove down the road and turned to her work. The rooster was heavy. She dragged him by his feet to the back of the barn. Using the shovel she had killed him with, she dug a hole and laid Sam in it. As she shoveled dirt over him, she watched the beautiful red feathers disappear. She knelt down and pulled out one long feather with iridescent green flecks on the end, a souvenir for her sister.

Five days later Easter Sunday dawned rosy and clear. Iris smelled cinnamon rolls and hopped out of bed. Her Easter dress hung on her closet door. She could hardly wait to dress in her new clothes. She had tried on the dress while her mother fitted it, and she had tried on her shoes in the store in

Rochester; but today she would tie up her hair with new ribbons and feel like a princess. Her grandmother had sent a package of fabric in the mail for her mother to make Easter outfits. Iris' material was polished cotton, a wonderful shade of pale lavender. Her mother thought it matched her daughter's eyes. Merry's soft blue fabric had tiny white flowers printed on it, and Martha Rose's dress was white cotton eyelet.

Iris put on the dress, her new white socks and her patent leather shoes. Then she tied a purple satin sash around her waist and pulled her hair behind her ears with ribbon to match. Her hair reached below her shoulder blades. She ran down stairs and into her mother's room to see herself in the mirror. Today she would not race and dash about, not in this dress. She knew she would wear her winter coat over her clothes, but she would take her coat off as soon as she walked in the church door.

On Good Friday her father had told her mother, "You know, it could snow on Easter. I just want you to be prepared. It happens."

Her mother laughed, "Oh, Horace."

"It's true. I'm not teasing," he said.

Martha Rose sat at the table with a tea towel around her neck so she wouldn't spill on her new clothes. She looked like an angel in her white dress—well, an angel with a bandage on one side of her face covering her rooster bite and a black eye and purple-turning-green lump on her forehead on the other side. Iris tried hard to keep a straight face. "Hap-py Ea-ster," she called out.

Her mother smiled when she saw her. "Your dress turned out better than I dreamed. Horace, we're ready. You must come see your girls!"

Iris' father came in as she sat down to breakfast, and Merry skipped into the room in her blue dress with her white straw hat on.

Horace smiled at his family and said, "I declare, you're pretty as an Easter bouquet, all of you sitting there; and, Merry, you are finally the picture of health."

Laura Ellen poured coffee for him and set the warm rolls on the table in front of him. "Help yourself and pass these around," she instructed. "I'm going to get dressed. I can't let my girls outdo me."

Laura Ellen's mother sent her daughter a small piece of pink linen and a length of navy blue linen. Iris' mother puzzled over what to make for herself and decided on a simple pink blouse and straight navy skirt. Iris thought her mother looked like a young girl when she wore pink. When Laura Ellen left the room, Horace leaned across the table and whispered, "I have a surprise for your mother. Look."

He reached under his chair and pulled out a box, lifted the lid and held it so each girl could see inside. There was a bouquet of fragile silk flowers inside, with a pin on them so they could be worn like a corsage. "I always buy flowers for your mother at Easter, but this year they'd die outside before we got to church. This is the next best thing. Do you think she'll like them?"

"Oh, Daddy, let me smell them," said Martha Rose.

Her sisters laughed as her mother came in the kitchen with her purse and new white gloves. She smiled and turned around.

"What do you think? Do I look homemade?"

"Mother, you look like a bea-utiful, bea-utiful lady," sighed Merry.

Horace handed his wife the box, "Wear these and you will be picture perfect."

Laura Ellen lifted out the silk flowers. There were pale violets with dark green leaves, lily-of-the-valley and tiny pink roses. "These are perfect, Horace!"

She lifted her head, touched the corner of one eye with her gloved hand and said, "Are we ready for church?" She untied Martha Rose's bib and pulled her youngest child's chair back from the table. "How are you feeling, Sweetheart?" she asked.

"Good. Let's go look at people dressed up. They can look at us. Then these will be old clothes, and nobody will look at nobody," declared Martha Rose.

*****

A week after Easter Iris was on the back steps with a piece of bread in one hand and a hunk of cheese in the other. Above the barn's double door, there was a hay loft, twenty feet off the ground. She heard singing and knew that Martha Rose was in the hay again, looking for mice.

She got up and walked to the barn, calling, "Martha Rosie Posie, Martha Rosie!" There was no answer, so she went into the barn and stood at the bottom of the ladder that led to the loft. "Martha Rose? You're not supposed to be up there." Still no answer, so she climbed the ladder until she saw her sister sitting on a stack of hay with a cookie in her hand. "Martha Rose! Didn't you hear me?" she asked.

"I heared you," she replied.

"Mother doesn't want you up there. Come down," commanded Iris.

Martha Rose stood up, "Watch this," she said and climbed onto a tall stack of hay. "I made a slide." She sat down and pushed with her hands and came sliding down towards her big sister.

"Martha Rose, you come down this minute," said Iris.

"One more slide," pleaded Martha Rose as her short legs climbed the steep stack of smoothed hay. "It's fun!"

The little girl lay down on her stomach this time and gave herself a push as down she came. Before Iris could stop her, she slid right into a post that went from the barn floor to the ceiling. Her head made a sickening crack.

Iris ran up the ladder, "Oh, Martha Rose!"

Her little sister tried to sit up and fell back.

Iris scooped her up and went to the ladder. "I can't carry you."

Martha Rose tried to stand up, but sat down heavily on her bottom. "Iris, I'm turning 'round."

"Listen to me, you! Stay right here and don't move. I'm

going to get Mother. I mean it; don't move."

Iris scrambled down the ladder, out of the barn, yelling for her mother.

Laura Ellen came out the back door and followed Iris to the ladder in the barn.

"Oh, good gracious! Martha Rose, what have you done now?"

Martha Rose lay on the hay. A bump was beginning to swell over her right eye.

Iris explained, "She was in the barn by herself, sliding on the hay. I told her to come down, but she wouldn't."

Her mother picked up the child. "This looks awful."

"I think she's pretending," said Iris. "She spoke to me just a minute ago."

Laura Ellen held Martha Rose with one arm and climbed carefully down the ladder. At the bottom of the ladder she shifted her daughter's weight, and Martha's head dangled over her shoulder. "She's not pretending now. She's knocked herself out! Get your father."

Iris ran down the drive and across the two-lane road to the field where she knew her father was working. He saw her come running and waved. As soon as she reached him, she blurted out, "Martha Rose . . . . again."

Before she could get her breath, her father was sprinting across the field towards the house. Holding her pounding chest with her hands, Iris followed.

Laura Ellen and Martha Rose were in the car as they came up the drive. "Get in," she called to her husband. "We need to get to Dr. Brenna's quickly. Iris, you and Merry wait here. We'll call." Then they were gone.

Iris found Merry in her bedroom drawing the dolls she'd posed on her bed. "Merry! Didn't you hear all that noise?"

"Was it Martha Rose again? Well? What happened?"

"How can you be so calm?" Iris fumed. "Martha Rose may have a concussion. She was talking to me, then she lay down and now she's unconscious!"

Merry put her doll down. "Why does Martha Rose always get hurt?"

"Daddy says she's a tomboy," Iris replied.

"We should go downstairs and wait," said Merry.

A basket of wet laundry sat on the kitchen table. "I'm going to hang these up," said Iris. She picked up the basket, balanced it on her hip and went out the back door. Merry followed. Soon the long clothes line was full of sheets and pillow cases flapping in the cool April breeze. Her mother had washed the curtains from Martha Rose's bedroom, and they jerked and tugged at the clothes pins.

They reminded Iris of her little sister, always pulling and tugging to run away and play. Iris should have stopped Martha Rose from taking that last slide. It was her fault. And before Sam had bitten her little sister, Iris should have taken her seriously. She should have kept Martha Rose from getting hurt twice.

Merry ran inside to answer the phone. She hollered, "Dr. Brenna called. They just got there. Martha Rose has a concuxion and is throwing up. If we get scared, Mother says we should go to Laughing Sky's."

Iris felt the cold feeling she had when she saw Martha Rose motionless in the hay. "Let's go."

The two girls held hands and ran across the pasture. Their frequent visits had worn a path. Dandelions and grass grew on each side of the worn track.

Laughing Sky was on her porch reading when the girls ran up the steps. Merry pointed to Iris and breathlessly said, "You tell."

Iris blurted, "Martha Rose has a concussion! She slid down a haystack into a post, head first!" Tears stung her eyes. "I was right there and she wouldn't stop. She has a lump on her head and she got knocked out!" She was crying hard now.

Laughing Sky reached for Iris and held her while she sobbed. Merry began to cry, also, and soon the young woman had both arms around the girls. "Let's go to your house and wait," she said. "Waiting is the very hardest part."

An hour later the Oldsmobile came down the drive. Iris, Merry and Laughing Sky sat together on the back steps. Laura Ellen opened the car door. Martha Rose was asleep on her lap.

The bump on her head was purple and stuck out like a goose egg. Her mother spoke, "We have to keep your sister quiet for three days. She'll sleep a lot. Dr. Brenna says she has a mild concussion, but she was very lucky it wasn't worse."

Horace took the little girl from Laura Ellen and carried her in the house, upstairs to her room. Iris followed, leaving Merry and Laughing Sky in the kitchen with her mother. Her father laid the child down and took off her shoes. Iris covered her sister with a blanket from the foot of the bed, pulled up a chair and sat watching her sister.

"What are you doing, Iris?" asked her father.

"I'm going to stay here until she wakes up," she explained.

"You don't have to do that."

"Yes, I do. I want to be the first person she sees when she wakes up. I have to tell her I'm sorry."

Horace bent over and looked at his oldest girl. "Sorry for what?" he asked.

"Sorry I didn't stop her." Iris covered her face with her hands and began to cry, pressing her fists to her eyes. "Oh, Daddy! I should have stopped her."

Horace put his arms around his daughter. "Iris, your sister is an adventuress. You are not going to be able to save her from a lot of things. She's going to learn the hard way. I doubt that you could have done one single thing to keep her from that last slide, and you know you *are* her hero for whacking Sam!"

Iris smiled and tasted her salty tears. "You go downstairs, Daddy. I'm going to stay and wait for our tomboy to wake up."

*****

Iris watched her sister breathe. Martha Rose's chest rose and fell in an even rhythm. Once she gave a shuddering sigh, and Iris leaned forward to see if she would wake up. There

89

were bits of hay in Martha Rose's hair and Iris began to pick them out. Her sister was a mess. Both of her knees were skinned and scabbed over, and there was a bruise on one shin. Her rooster bite was still dark red and would leave a scar. Iris shook her head and settled back in the chair. What would ever become of Martha Rose?

"Which is you?"

Iris lifted her head. The bedroom was almost dark. She had fallen asleep on watch.

"Which is you?" Martha Rose repeated.

Iris leaned over the bed. "Martha Rose, don't you ever scare me like that again."

Martha Rose put her hand to her forehead and felt the lump. "Ouch, ouch. Is that me sticking out?" she asked.

"It certainly is. You silly girl, you knocked yourself out. Now you have to stay in bed for three days." Iris waggled a finger at her sister. "I am going to stay here and see that you do."

Martha Rose's eyes brimmed with tears. "Don't be mad. I got tears in my ears 'cause you makin' me cry."

Iris jumped up. "I'll get Mother," she said.

"No," whined her sister. "I want you. Mama jiggles me." Martha Rose held out one dusty hand, yawned and closed her eyes.

Iris looked at the plump hand in hers. Martha Rose needed to clean her fingernails. Actually Martha Rose needed a bath. Iris decided that the next time her sister woke up, she would run a warm bath in the tub, use the special soap her grandmother had sent and scrub her sister good. Martha Rose had said she wanted Iris to stay. If Iris couldn't save her little sister from her wild escapades, she could at least be there to comfort her after they were over.

Chapter Ten

MAY

The red wagon was full of picnic supplies. Julie had spent the night and carried a small sack of bar cookies so they wouldn't crumble. Merry followed with Cookie at her heels as Martha Rose ran ahead, picking buttercups. Horace came out of the barn as they headed for the pasture path. "Where are my fair maidens going with lunch?" he asked.

"This is not your lunch, Daddy. This is my lunch," answered Martha Rose, "An' we're goin' to Laughing Sky's cabin. Girls only. Except Oscar."

"Martha Rose, you tell everything. I only said that Oscar *might* come," hollered Iris. She waved at her father, "Good bye, Daddy. Mother thought this up. She says you need to talk. I suppose she thinks I shouldn't be included on anything important, even if I am the oldest." She thought to herself: *and I'm not as important as I thought I was!* Iris scuffed a patch of grass with her shoe.

Julie hung back, red-faced. She had never talked back to her father like that.

Iris was so . . . emotional.

Iris' father said, "We'll tell you about it when you get home. Don't ruin the day with that scowl. You'll get wrinkles."

Merry and Cookie caught up with her. Merry called out, "Come on, Iris. Let's have fun."

"Yeah, and let Mother and Daddy make all the important decisions," said Iris.

As soon as Laughing Sky's cabin came in sight, Martha Rose began to yell, "Yoo-hoo! Yoo-hoo! Are you ready? We almost dere."

"Martha Rose, you are going to drive me crazy before we

91

get there," commented Iris.

"Sour puss," called Martha Rose. "I havin' a nic-pic."

Laughing Sky walked down the steps of her cabin. "My goodness, I heard you all the way across the pasture! Hello, Julie, I'm so happy you can join us. Martha Rose, you look hungry. Let's find a shady spot by the creek." Laughing Sky placed a sack on top of the pile of picnic goodies in the wagon.

"Let's walk across the rocks and sit on the other side of the creek," suggested Merry. Cookie splashed through the water, walking up and down the creek, drinking and snuffling in the cool shallows.

"And how do you think I would get this wagon over there?" questioned Iris.

Laughing Sky looked at Iris' face, now pink with the sun and work of pulling the wagon. "I'll take a turn with the wagon, if you like," she offered.

Iris kept her grip on the handle and shook her head.

Julie ran ahead and called out, "Here! Come here and see this!"

The spot was made for a picnic. A clear area where moss led down to the creek was surrounded by trees and a few smooth stones. Merry sat down on one and Cookie walked up from the creek, shaking water as she came.

"That dog is grinning," said Laughing Sky. "Iris, how's this spot?"

"Okay," said Iris, slinging the wagon handle down and plopping on the grass. "Merry, you unpack. I'm hot."

"I'll show you what I brought," said Laughing Sky as she opened her satchel. "Martha Rose, what did you bring?"

Martha Rose took six big apples out of a bag and put them on the ground.

Iris sighed, "You have to get the tablecloth."

"We ain't got no table," said the little girl.

"Say, 'we haven't got any table,'" corrected Iris.

"That's what I said," her sister answered.

"All right, girls," began Laughing Sky. "Iris, what *is* the matter?" She moved close to her young friend. "This isn't like you."

"Aw, Mother and Daddy are having a talk right now without us." Iris blinked to stop the tears that threatened to spill. "I know what they're talking about. Mother wants to go back to Virginia, and she doesn't want us to know, so she packed us off on a picnic to convince Daddy we made a mistake moving here." She looked at Julie, then Laughing Sky. "I don't know whether we're staying or going. Mother keeps changing her mind. I wish she'd decide! Since Grandpa died, she's wanted to go back something terrible."

"Isn't your mother going to Virginia this summer?"

"She said she was. She doesn't think we can get along, doesn't think our crop will be any good, doesn't think I work hard enough, or that I can help Daddy, and she doesn't think I should go riding with Oscar. She doesn't want me to say anything, and she doesn't want me to do anything either!"

Laughing Sky raised her eyebrows and said to Julie, Merry and Martha Rose, who stood next to the wagon, listening. "Sit down, girls. Maybe we can think of a way to help." Martha Rose patted Cookie who had fallen asleep on a patch of sunny grass.

Laughing Sky said, "Iris, this doesn't sound like your mother, but remember, she's been through a series of shocks this winter. She wasn't able to go to her father's funeral, and that must have made her very sad. I know that when I get sad, sometimes I act like I'm angry; and when I wish I could cry, I make a fuss instead."

"Mother doesn't cry," said Merry.

"Yeah, an' we jumped in bed and cried all day when Grandpa died," added Martha Rose.

"Sometimes people think that if they start to cry, they won't stop. Remember your mother's had a terrible year," said Laughing Sky.

"So what can we do about it?" asked Iris in a rough voice.

"Let's take her some of those yellow flowers down by the creek," offered Julie.

93

"Those are marsh marigolds and that would be a great idea," said Laughing Sky. "I think I hear Oscar's pony."

Oscar and Blue appeared at a trot, and as they came near, Oscar slid off the pony's back and led Blue to the water's edge for a drink. Cookie lifted her head, sniffed and went back to sleep.

"Did you save me any lunch?" asked Oscar.

"We ain't even got started," said Martha Rose. "What'd you bring me?"

"Let's put everything on the cloth," Laughing Sky suggested, "and help ourselves."

After the contributions were laid out, Martha Rose said, "That's a lot of nic-pic!"

Iris looked at the cheese sandwiches, apples, a jar of her mother's potato salad, Oscar's hard-boiled eggs, slices of ham on biscuits, Laughing Sky's oatmeal cookies and Julie's lemon bars. "I think I just got an appetite," she said.

Oscar sat close enough to Cookie to slip the puppy bits of his lunch. "You looked like you were having a church meeting when I rode up. What's going on?"

"Mother and Daddy are having a conference without us. They are discussing going back to Virginia. Mother doesn't think anything good will ever happen here," explained Iris.

Oscar chewed his cookie and said, "There's not a thing you can do about that."

"Oh, Oscar!" wailed Iris. "You're no help."

"It is true. When my mother died, everyone wanted to make me happy. I got presents from people I hardly knew. We were invited to dinner, and everybody in Harmony brought food. People wrote letters and sent cards, my teachers were very nice to me and my friends were careful around me. They even let me win at games! It was awful." He reached for another cookie.

"What happened?" asked Iris. "What made you change?"

Her friend looked steadily at her. "What makes you think I've changed?"

"You're no help at all."

"Well, thanks!" Oscar shook his head until his hair flew straight out.

Merry spoke up, "Iris is making everybody mad."

Iris stood up. "I am not! Listen, do you want to go back to Virginia? I want to stay here . . . I think. At least, I want to know what's going to happen. This back and forth stuff is driving me crazy. I don't know if I should bother to make friends or work hard at school. Why should I? I might not be here next year."

Julie said, "You have your hands on your hips again. That's a bad sign."

Iris scowled at her.

"I have an idea," said Laughing Sky.

"Let's hear it. Nobody else has anything smart to add," said Iris.

"I disagree with you. Oscar has some good suggestions. I think you should listen to him. He knows what your mother is going through. If your mother decides to go home for a visit, I could come and help. We can suggest this to your father, but first you all need to get an agreement from your mother."

Iris nodded her head, "Sometimes we have a family circle where we go around the table and tell one thing that happened in the day that was good and one thing that was bad. Do you think we could do that?"

"Yes!" said Laughing Sky. "You could tell your mother how sad you are about your grandpa and that you and your sisters would like to hear the discussion about staying or leaving. You do know, though, in the end it will be up to the grown-ups."

"Let's do it tonight, Iris. As soon as we get back, find Daddy and set it up," said Merry.

"All right," agreed Iris with a sigh. She held up a stick. "I don't know if this is a good idea or not, but right now anybody for a game of chase the stick?" Cookie's nose went up and the dog was on her feet in a second. Iris threw the stick into the creek and Cookie bounded after it, splashing Oscar, who laughed and ran to throw the stick as soon as Cookie laid it on the bank.

Iris, Julie and Laughing Sky sat with their feet in the creek. Laughing Sky untangled Iris' hair and braided it in one long plait. Iris asked, "Why won't Mother let me go riding with Oscar? I always have to take sisters along. Sometime, just sometime I'd like to explore without them."

"Your mother is uneasy here. You've told me about your town in Virginia, how you had friends next door. She wants you to be safe," answered her friend. Julie nodded.

The wagon was empty now, so Martha Rose pulled it home. Oscar mounted Blue, took off with a wave and hollered, "See you later!"

*****

As the girls walked home, they made plans. Merry picked fuzzy pussy willows and Julie found two early daffodils in bloom. When they arrived, Iris carried the empty picnic basket into the kitchen.

Her mother sat in a rocker, reading. As the four girls came in, she looked up from her book. "My goodness, you must have had a wonderful time! I thought you were going to stay for dinner."

Merry came in with her flowers. "Mother, I made you a bouquet."

Their mother's face brightened, "Now that's spring! Daffodils."

"We can say these are for Grandpa too," added Merry.

Iris saw her mother duck her head in a now-familiar motion and realized this was her mother's way of hiding her emotions.

"We didn't bring any leftovers," Iris said. "It was a great day for a picnic."

Her mother said, "Iris, Merry, come here. Your father and I want to talk to you tonight after dinner. You've been so brave during our adventure in the Midwest that we want to include you in our discussion about fall."

Iris and Merry looked at their mother and kept their faces serious. Iris spoke up, "Well, what a good idea. What do you think, Merry?"

Merry pretended to consider her sister's question and answered, "Yes. That *is* a good idea. I'm so glad you thought of it, Mother."

Julie stood quietly next to the table.

*****

After dinner, the girls hurried to clear the table. Julie's father had picked her up in his truck on the way to town. There were no fusses about who would wash or dry, and they took what jobs needed to be done. Horace shook the tablecloth and spread it on the table again, with Merry's flowers as a centerpiece. Everyone pulled out their chairs and sat down at the table together.

Iris thought they'd never start. First her father got up and brought a pad and pencil to the table. Then Martha Rose had to go to the bathroom. Then her mother wanted a glass of water. Finally they were all together.

As Iris looked around the table at her family, she knew that tonight would make a difference. Her mother looked beautiful. Laura Ellen wore her long hair in a bun at the nape of her neck and had taken off her apron, something she hardly ever did. She had on a blue blouse and her cheeks were pink. Even her father looked special. He had wet and combed his pale blond hair and replaced his plaid flannel work shirt with a blue Sunday shirt, but no tie.

He began, "This family circle will come to order! Your mother and I had a long talk today. Every time we thought we had reached a decision, we wondered, 'What would Iris say, or what about Merry and Martha Rose?' so we quit talking and decided to ask you in person. Your mother pointed out how much help each of you has been since we left Virginia. I get so busy that I hardly sleep, so I have missed out on a lot. You'll have to forgive me.

"What we need to do now is talk. Here it is May. The ground is warming, the tractor's running, the first crop of wheat is in the ground and the corn planting is close to being finished. What do you think? Your mother's as homesick as a young calf. Our little house in Virginia is only rented for one year. We can go back. Speak up; let us know what you think."

Martha Rose asked, "Do we haf to raise our hands?"

"No, Sweetheart. Did you have something to say?" asked her father.

"Yes!" said Martha Rose in her biggest voice. "We can't leaf Cookie!"

"We'd never do that," he said.

"I want to go back to Vaginya with Cookie!" yelled Martha Rose.

Iris stood up and pointed at her little sister. "You do not!" she yelled.

"Iris, sit down," said her father. "Each of us has a chance to talk."

"What about you, Merry Columbine?" asked her mother. "How do you feel about Harmony?"

Merry broke into a big grin. "Mother, I feel fine! I was sick for a long time and I had you to myself. I'm thinking I was a lot of trouble and you must be worn out. I think you should go visit Grannie in Virginia, then come back."

Laura Ellen took a handkerchief out of her skirt pocket and dabbed her eyes, "That is the dearest thing I have ever heard you say, Merry."

Iris spoke up, "What a good idea! Perfect, Merry."

Iris continued, "I miss my friends; I do. I miss Grandma; I even miss my street! It sounds silly but I do. I miss the trees, how they make an arch over the hot street. I will always be homesick, just like Daddy was homesick for Minnesota. Whatever we do, somebody's going to be homesick."

Martha Rose began kicking the table leg. "I'm goin' with Mama and I'm not coming back."

Iris got ready to stand up, then sat down again. "I can't believe you. You love it here. Oscar's your best friend. The barn is your favorite spot on this earth. You're just being mean because you know I want to stay!"

"I-don't-like-that-barn." Martha Rose had her arms crossed over her chest. She pointed to her rooster bite and fading bruise.

"That's it. I quit," said Iris and stood up from the table.

"Please sit down, Iris," her mother grabbed Iris' hand. "I want you all to know that your father and I have decided that I *will* visit Virginia. "Iris, you are getting to be a good cook, and Martha Rose isn't a baby anymore."

"I ain't been a baby for a year," crowed Martha Rose.

Iris added, "Laughing Sky will help."

Horace said, "We called Grandma, and she said June would be a good time."

Iris looked at her mother, "What about when you get back? Will we stay?"

"Yes," her mother answered. She sat still, tears running down her face.

"I not staying." Martha Rose's face was red. She reached out and punched Iris in the shoulder.

Her father took the little girl in his lap. "You are staying. We can't get along without you!"

Martha Rose began to cry.

Iris reached for her mother and hugged her hard. "We'll be so good while you're gone. I'll watch Martha Rose every minute. I'll write you a letter every day. Will you take one to Dorothy, and would you take our rhubarb jam to our neighbor, Mr. Broome?"

Her father put his hands on Iris' shoulder, "Let your mother cry and don't bother her with details. This is a happy cry."

Laura Ellen held out her arms, "All of you, come here." The girls crowded close, and their mother pulled them to her. "I don't know how I will stay away from you for two weeks, but I'm going to Virginia and we're staying in Minnesota!"

Chapter Eleven

JUNE

As soon as Iris awoke, she realized *this* was the day. She was sad and excited at the same time. She heard her parents talking in the kitchen beneath her room. Today they would drive her mother to Rochester to take the train to Richmond. She slipped out of bed and began to dress.

In the kitchen Horace and Laura Ellen looked up at Iris as she came in and sat at the table. Her parents were holding hands! She leaned over and kissed her mother's cheek. Her mother had on her navy blue Easter skirt and a white blouse. "I better get out of these work clothes so I can take you to the depot in style," Horace said and left the room.

Laura Ellen and her daughter sat in silence, and then her mother said, "I made oatmeal. You get started and I'll get your sisters."

When the family was dressed and had eaten breakfast, Iris' father put his wife's tan suitcase in the trunk of the car. Her mother stood in the kitchen, pulling on her gloves, looking around like she'd forgotten something. The little girls were already in the car. "I think we should go, Mother," Iris suggested.

"I know, I know. I can't believe the day has arrived. I've looked forward to this and now I don't want to go."

"Mother, think of Grandma!"

Her mother gave her a smile, took a deep breath and said, "You're right. Goodbye, kitchen. I'm off."

The Andersens sat on long wooden benches at the Rochester train station, waiting for the train that would take their mother to Chicago. Next she would have to change trains and get on another one that went to Washington, D.C., and then on to Richmond. Even Martha Rose was quiet. Laura Ellen held her purse in her lap with her train ticket in one hand.

Horace kept up a steady stream of talk. "Laughing Sky will be an enormous help. I'll help Earl cultivate his wheat—that should take two days—then he'll help me. He doesn't talk much. We get along fine. Oh, and we'll all keep Martha Rose out of the hay loft." He laughed a dry laugh and the rest of the family just looked at him. Finally he fell silent.

Merry leaned forward, "Listen!"

Sure enough, Iris heard the distant rumble of the train. Her family stood up and went out the swinging doors to the platform. Her father carried her mother's suitcase and set it beside the tracks. "Stand back, Martha Rose. Put your fingers in your ears like this," he demonstrated.

The little girl poked her fingers in her ears as instructed.

Down the track puffed the giant black engine, slowing to a screech in bursts of steam. Iris looked at her youngest sister. Martha Rose's mouth was open in a scream, but Iris couldn't hear a thing. It seemed like the train would never stop. The engine passed them and then the coal car and several passenger cars. It slowed to a halt, clouds of steam billowing.

A handsome young man dressed in a suit stepped off the train. Iris wondered why he was in Harmony. Then the conductor, in a striped vest and shiny hat, stepped off the passenger car and placed a stepping stool next to the entrance. "All aboard!" he shouted.

Iris' mother stepped forward with her ticket.

"Wait!" called her husband. "Aren't you going to kiss us?"

Her mother turned and there were tears in her eyes. Iris heard her mother say, "Horace, I don't think I can. Don't make me."

He took his wife in his arms. "You don't have to do anything you don't want to. If you don't want to go, you can turn your ticket in and we can get a little of the money back."

Iris took her mother's arm. "What will Grandmother think? You'll be glad you went when you get there. We'll miss you but we'll be fine. I promise."

Merry added, "We'll be waiting right here when you come back."

Her mother lifted her head, "All right. I'm going. Don't say goodbye. I am going to step on that stool and get on that train right now." She stood perfectly still.

"All aboard," the conductor rang out. He looked at Iris' mother and said, "Young lady, if you're going to Chicago, step right up here."

"My mama is going to see our Grannie," Martha Rose explained.

The conductor turned to Laura Ellen, "Well, you might as well come on, 'cause we're about to pull out. Let me help you with that bag."

She was gone.

The train began to move with a jerk and clank. The engine pulled forward and the car with Iris' mother in it followed. Horace held Martha Rose on his shoulders so she could wave, but no one could see where her mother had found a seat. A man waved from a window and Martha Rose asked, "Does he know me?"

The ride home was quiet. Iris thought of the long journey ahead for her mother. Then she smiled as she imagined the greeting her mother would get in Richmond.

As her father pulled into the drive of their house, Iris looked at the rose bushes along the fence and remembered the first time she had seen them, almost a year ago.

Horace and his girls entered the empty kitchen. Martha Rose piped up, "I want some water. Get me some." She was too short to reach the faucet.

Her father replied, "Well, Little-Bit, we're going to pull your mother's chair close to the sink, and you can stand on it and reach the faucet just fine. We won't have to wait on you." He looked at his girls. "This is going to be a long two weeks."

*****

Iris' father loved to tell stories about Joshua, the farm's Belgian work horse. Joshua was eighteen hands high at his withers. At first he terrified Iris. Now she loved the docile animal. To her Joshua was the very best thing about Minnesota. She liked to brush him in the winter, and on long summer afternoons, the dim barn was a cool place to be. She combed and untangled his mane and braided it once with only a few snorts and foot-shuffling from the horse.

Iris liked to climb the slats in Joshua's stall and sit on his broad back. He was so wide her legs stuck out on both sides. When he was in his stall, Iris could balance easily on his back and stare at the rafters of the barn. There was nothing like the quiet strength of the big horse. Her father had shown her how to harness him, and she loved to lead the huge animal around the yard.

In his old age Joshua had become stubborn. In the fall he had pulled Iris slowly to an apple tree and began to munch, or he would lead her to a particularly juicy patch of grass. Then it was Iris' turn to be patient, and she would stand and wait until the horse had his fill.

Iris' dream was a pony of her own. Every Christmas "Pony" was at the top of her Santa List. She imagined herself trotting, jumping over logs in the forest, her hair blowing in the wind, her body leaning forward.

At least she had Joshua. One morning her father agreed that she could ride him bareback down the drive and across the pasture to visit Laughing Sky. The day was sunny with clouds puffy as her mother's meringue. Iris and Joshua set out on a slow walk down the drive. Joshua had one speed: plodding. Iris turned and waved to her father, and he waved back, then went to his barn chores.

At the end of the drive Iris pulled on the harness to turn Joshua towards Laughing Sky's house, but he twisted his head, looked at her, slowed to a stop, still as a statue.

"Joshua," Iris said in exasperation, "There's nothing to see, just cornfields and a road to nowhere. Turn around."

Across the black macadam road, a far as Iris could see, stretched the new corn crop, pale green and tender. There was not a car in sight. Iris knew she could slip off the horse's back and lead him back to the barn, but giving up was not her way. Joshua shifted his weight and looked across the road.

Iris gazed at the field in front of her, as flat as a checkerboard. She missed Virginia's rolling hills. Storms could be seen for miles away bearing down on them. The wind blew and blew and no hill or tree slowed it down.

Iris thought of her house in Virginia and the bedroom she shared with Merry. Iris sniffed and her eyes smarted. She wiped a tear from her cheek with the back of her hand, as Joshua began to move. He walked stiffly and deliberately across the two lane road and stood at the edge of the corn field. Iris jerked the reins, "Joshua, get back to the road. Joshua!"

Now she knew what the horse had in mind. The shoots of corn were too much temptation. Carefully Joshua nibbled one shoot of corn. His large hooves left deep imprints in the soft black soil.

Iris turned around and looked for her father, but there was no sign of him. She tugged desperately on the reins and cried, "Gee! Gee! Don't you take another bite!" The horse methodically moved on to another plant. Iris slid off the side of the horse, crying in earnest, "Joshua, come home! Daddy will never forgive us." She tugged on the harness with all her strength, but the big animal kept mowing down the row of corn.

From behind Iris heard a horse galloping and someone yelling, "Hey! Hey!" It was Oscar; he was bolting towards them on Blue. He leaped from his horse and slapped Joshua on the rump! "Get! Get!" he cried.

Surprised at the outburst, Joshua gazed longingly at the corn shoots, then ambled across the road, down the drive to the barn. Iris followed, weeping. Oscar walked beside her, leading Blue by a rope.

"Iris, you don't need to cry. Joshua didn't do much damage.

There's no harm done." He hurried to keep up with her.

Barely able to see through her tears, Iris began to run. Then there was her father, standing tall in front of her. He grabbed her and put his arms around her. "Iris, my big girl. Don't cry so. I saw what was happening and was on my way down the drive when Oscar sent Joshua to the barn." Horace held Iris at arm's length and looked at her. "You know Joshua couldn't resist that new corn any more than you can resist a plate of cookies. It was too much for him."

Iris raised her face to her father, "Oh, Daddy, I want to go home." She buried her face in her father's rough shirt.

Horace shrugged his shoulders, "I thought that of all of us here, you loved the farm the best."

Iris looked at her father. Oscar stood nearby. "I thought so too," said Iris, "but today I was thinking about our tulip bed at home and my cozy room with Merry. . . Daddy, I never wanted a room to myself." She began to cry again. "I've never been so lonesome in all my life."

Horace looked at Oscar as if asking for help. "When my girls are unhappy," he said, "I feel like a jelly fish."

Oscar's troubled eyes began to gleam. "Iris, I know where there is the most beautiful flower in the world in bloom right now. They don't grow in Virginia, so you've never seen one. There's a secret place . . . no one, well, no one alive knows about it but me." He held out a hand, "Let me show you."

Iris lifted her head from her father's chest, and he nodded, "Go see Oscar's secret place," he said. "Maybe it will take your mind off those tulips."

Iris released her arms from her father's waist and swiped at her eyes with her shirt sleeve. "May I go by myself?" she asked. Her father nodded yes. She took Oscar's hand. It was almost as large as her father's, but bony, like she was holding a strong bird in her hand.

Oscar walked over to Blue, who had followed them up the drive. He said, "I'll give you a leg up," and she swung up and onto the pony's back. Then he jumped up behind her and they trotted down the drive. Neither of them spoke. Iris sniffled occasionally. Blue kept to the side of the road until they had traveled about a mile. Then Oscar directed the pony through some brush until they came to a rough path. Iris could barely see her farmhouse roof in the distance and heard water trickling nearby.

"Is there a creek here?" she asked in surprise.

"This is the most beautiful creek you'll ever see," answered Oscar. "It leads to the Iowa River and goes past the limestone caves. When your family moved in, I was afraid you'd go exploring and find my secret place."

"Oh, you know Mother. She wanted us in plain view. I couldn't go off on my own for anything," said Iris.

The path followed the widening creek and moss covered the bank. Ferns grew in the crook of the bank where rocks and roots of small trees forced the creek to bend and twist.

Oscar tugged Blue to a stop and slid off. Iris followed his movements and carefully slipped to the ground. "Now we walk," explained her friend. He tied Blue's rope to a small poplar tree near the creek and continued down the path. The trees were taller, and the creek cut deeply into the earth.

Oscar stopped and looked at her. "You'll have to promise never to bring anyone here, not your sisters, not even Julie. The water gets deep after a heavy rain, and there are rattlesnakes near." He walked on quietly. "At certain places the creek disappears. It seeps underground and goes into the caves. There's a lake down there not far from where we are." The path opened onto a wide grassy area. Oscar stopped and turned to her. "Promise. Tell no one."

"I promise," said Iris, crossing her heart.

Oscar pushed aside low branches and Iris followed. Except for the creek's music and birds twittering, there was silence in the glade as peaceful as night. The trees opened up and there was a grass-covered circle. Oscar sat on a boulder in the center of the grass and motioned Iris to climb up next to him. The boulder was shaped like a rounded chair, and the bowl of it held the two of them perfectly.

"I don't know anyone who has been here except my mother and me, and now you. Look," he pointed ahead. "There they are. Lady Slippers."

Iris drew in her breath. Slender stems trembled in the breeze. Glossy leaves fanned out at their base, and at the top of the stems were orchids in palest powder pink with distinct slipper shapes. The toes dangled and danced with showy petals falling behind.

"They're magic!" she breathed. "Magic." She looked at Oscar. His eyes, darkened in the shade, were deep blue.

They sat together. Iris could hear her breath coming in and out, and it seemed the world quieted to listen with her.

She turned to her friend, "Tell me about your mother."

Oscar closed his eyes and remained silent.

Iris pulled her legs up and rested her chin on her knees. A breeze blew the Lady Slippers, and they jerked and swayed. Out of the corner of her eye, Iris could see Oscar's brown hands hanging off his bent knees. She had never known a place like this. These were fairy shoes and the moss was crushed emerald. This was a magic circle, like the ones she'd read about in fairy tales. She could imagine elves . . .

"She had eyes like mine," Oscar began. "She was taller than my father, and her hair was straight and fine like silk. My daddy used to say it was the color of spun gold, but I never saw spun gold. She tied it up around her head in braids like a crown. She was a teacher on the reservation in Cass County when my father met her. Her parents didn't want her to marry an Ojibway, but they did like my father. Anyway, they got married. Mom got sick during the epidemic two years ago and died in three days. Two hundred people on the reservation died."

Iris listened to the wind rustle the cottonwood trees. They seemed to whisper two hundred, two hundred. Clouds formed overhead and the breeze grew chilly. The bright green moss turned dull without the sun.

"A front's moving in," said Oscar. "Let's head back before rain."

As Oscar helped her onto the pony, she asked, "Isn't the weather wonderful? In Virginia it would stay the same for days and days. Out here it changes every hour. And you know what else is great? It's so flat you can see it coming. I love these fields with the wind blowing."

Oscar looked at her before swinging up behind her, "I thought you were homesick. Your mind changes as fast as the weather."

Iris laughed. "I was homesick. Thinking of mother in Richmond and me here made me sad. I never want to leave Harmony!"

*****

The days without her mother dragged by. Iris would enter the kitchen, expecting to see her mother finishing up one meal or beginning another. The room was empty without her. Laughing Sky helped keep the girls amused. They had picnics and made bouquets of wildflowers for the house. Martha Rose had not skinned her knees once.

Tonight the girls and their friend planned to sleep under the stars. Iris carried blankets through the kitchen and out the back door. Merry picked out a level spot near the kitchen garden. Martha Rose came around the side of the house with three dolls and a teddy bear and laid them on her blanket.

Iris watched her little sister settle her charges. How could Martha Rose be so gentle and then so wild? Cookie sniffed, curled up and lay down on Iris' blanket. "No, Cookie, this isn't your spot." She patted the grass next to her blanket. "Dogs don't belong on the bed."

"Now you sound like mother," said Martha Rose, "and that is not a bed. It is a blanket. How is Cookie s'posed to know?" The little girl pulled a blanket over her body.

"What are you doing?" asked Iris.

"Goin' to bed," replied her sister.

108

"It is 4:00 in the afternoon," said Iris.

Martha Rose threw back the blanket. "You are absodootly right," she said as she jumped up and ran away. Cookie followed.

Iris sat on the pallet she had made for the night. She thought of Oscar, whose mother would never come home. Tomorrow she and her sisters would go to Rochester again. The train would roar into the station; her mother would get off and they would all drive home. Everything would be the way it was supposed to be with her mother in the house or tending the garden and her father coming in from the field, hot and dusty. Her mother would greet him with a glass of lemonade.

*****

Laura Ellen returned to Harmony, bringing news from Dorothy and mementos that had belonged to their grandfather for the girls. When Horace opened the box and unwrapped the packaging, Iris' eyes fell on the wooden box where her grandpa kept his treasures. Her mother picked it up and handed it to her. "Iris, your Grannie remembered how you and Grandpa used to sit on the floor for hours when you were little, picking through these."

Iris took the box in both hands, shook it gently and listened for the rattle and clatter inside. She ran upstairs to her room and sat on her bed with the box in front of her. She unhooked the clasp and opened the lid.

There they were! Her grandfather's prized marble collection. The cat's eyes were here, the steely, the aggies, the ones they had made up names for, like whirly and robin's egg. One by one she took each glass marble in her hand and squeezed her palm shut around it. They clicked together as she put them back in the box, handling them as if they were precious stones. She heard her mother's step as she entered the room.

"Mother, this is Grandpa's marble collection," Iris exclaimed.

"I know," her mother said. "Your Grannie also wants you to have this." Her mother held a gold bracelet in her hand. "It was an engagement gift from Grandpa to Grandma. See, it's engraved with your Grannie's initials and the date on the inside. It opens like this," Laura Ellen undid a tiny clasp and a hidden hinge opened the gold circle.

"How can she part with this?" asked Iris.

"Because she wants you to have it," answered her mother.

"I'm going to wear it when I get married," declared Iris, "and not until then. I'm going to write Grannie tonight. She will be so lonesome since you're gone. I'm going to write her every week."

"You are indeed my thoughtful one. I missed you every day, daughter."

"Mother, I missed you every day too. I'm glad, glad, glad you're home!"

Chapter Twelve

JULY

Iris watched as her mother supervised her father. Horace was packing cupcakes in a box for her mother to carry to a ladies' luncheon at the church. Wisps of Laura Ellen's black hair floated out of the bun she had pinned to the nape of her neck. No matter how carefully her mother brushed and pinned her hair, it escaped into loose unruly curls around her face.

As they carried the cupcakes to the car, Iris looked at the sky. "Mother, look at that color. I wish you hadn't promised the ladies to make dessert for their lunch today. I want you to come with us on our hike."

Her sisters stood at the back door with satchels that held lunch, sweaters and flashlights.

"Go on, Mama," pleaded Martha Rose.

"Martha Rose is just in a hurry to get started," Iris explained.

"I know. I know. Goodness, look at you all," said her mother.

"Beautiful, aren't we?" asked her father.

"Healthy, aren't we?" added Merry.

Iris' mother smiled at her tall husband, "Horace, do you worry when things go well? You know, the calm before the storm?"

"I'm not worried today," he replied.

"I am," chirped Martha Rose.

Her father sighed and turned to his wife. "Enjoy your lunch with the women. We'll tell you all about our adventure when you get back." He kissed his wife and opened the door to the car. "My, you look independent behind the wheel of that machine!"

Carol Pearce Bjorlie

Laura Ellen rolled her window down. "Do you have water? Merry, are those really the shoes you plan to wear hiking? Remember, Horace, we're going to get the heavy blankets and quilts down from the attic this afternoon."

"Mother!" exclaimed Merry.

"All right. All right. Goodbye." She waved as she drove down the drive.

Iris looked at her father. "Daddy, why are we getting the blankets down in July?"

He looked back at her with no expression on his face. "We're going to pack them."

The younger girls ran to the path that led to the pasture, then the creek. Martha Rose took the lead.

"Daddy, now you haf to tell us where we're goin'."

"You're right." He fell in step with her. "We're going to eat lunch by the creek and hike to the limestone caves and explore."

"Caves!" called Merry. "That's why we brought flashlights."

"Correct! And sweaters," he added.

"Why, Daddy, why did we bring s'veters?" asked Martha Rose.

"Because caves stay at a cool temperature all year round. You'll like it after our hot hike. My father used to take me to these caves."

"These must be the caves Oscar told me about," said Iris.

"How dark will it be?" asked Martha Rose.

"Pitch black dark. Dark as midnight. Dark as the inside of a sock," answered her father. "After lunch we can sit on the rocks, play in the water, have a look inside the largest cave and head home."

"I am not goin' in dat cave," stated Martha Rose.

"Martha Rose, I'll show you a secret river. These limestone caves are a wonder. You'll never see anything like it. Besides, you're not afraid of anything!"

"I am afraid of dat cave," said the little girl.

112

As they walked through the pasture, Merry moved closer to her father. A neighboring farmer's cows grazed here. "Daddy, are we safe in the middle of these cows?" she asked.

"They're big, aren't they?" he said. "They're gentle, though. They want to eat and be left alone."

"They are wooking at me," said Martha Rose.

"Look!" called Iris, who had walked ahead. "These trees mean we're almost at the creek."

Merry took her daddy's hand. "Are there snakes here?"

"Well, there are snakes, but they are as afraid of us as we are of them. I'm sure they heard us coming and are headed to Iowa about now."

"You never said anything about snakes," Merry said in a small voice.

When they reached the creek, the girls clambered over rocks, chased one another and jumped from boulder to boulder. Finally tired, Iris took off her shoes and dangled her tan legs in the cool water.

Her father called, "Anybody hungry?"

"Lunch!" yelled Martha Rose.

Between bites of her ham sandwich, Iris asked, "Which direction are the caves? How far are they? Let's eat fast and go."

"They aren't far at all. Past this bend we walk uphill a little." He patted Martha Rose on the head. "It's a climb, but this little rock-hopper will do fine."

"I'm a good hopper, I am," said Martha Rose, patting her chubby legs.

Merry stuffed her waxed paper into her sack and pulled out her flashlight and sweater. "I'm ready!"

The others picked up their sacks and followed her.

As the group started down the river path, Iris sang, "Oh, the bear went over the mountain, the bear went over the mountain, the bear went over the mountain . . . . to see what he could see."

Her father and sisters joined in the song and clambered over the warm rocks to the cave above.

Iris, Horace and Merry stood for a moment in front of the dark entrance. The opening was higher than their father. Honeysuckle vines grew around it and hung over the entrance. A draft from the cave kept them swaying.

Iris was the first to step inside. "It's cool already. Merry, come in."

Merry and her father put their sweaters on and followed Iris through the rocky entrance. Horace called to Martha Rose, who stood several yards from the cave. "Come on, Little One."

She did not budge.

"I'll carry you piggy-back," offered her father. He stretched out his hand to her.

The little girl took her father's hand, and he knelt to swing her up and onto his back. He crooked his arms around her dangling legs.

"Turn on your flashlights," he suggested, and he walked carefully through the entrance. The cave devoured the four Andersens.

"Everybody listen. Be absolutely still," he said.

There was a slow drip, drip, drip trickling noise.

Martha Rose whispered, "Dey got a leak in here."

"Water seeps through the roof of the cave and trickles down to join a lake in the cave," her father explained.

"I want to see it," said Iris. "Oscar says it disappears and reappears."

Martha Rose began to squirm, "I want to go back, Daddy." She clutched a fist full of her father's hair in her hands.

"Little One, if you don't let loose of my hair, you'll have a bald-headed daddy when we get home. Then we'll have some explaining to do to your mother." He bent over to avoid a low outcropping of rock.

"Martha Rose, this isn't going to work. I need you to walk. Here, I'll set you down."

The child began to shriek and struggle, kicking her father in the side in panic.

"Don't set me down! Don't do it!" she squealed.

114

Then Iris heard an odd sound. There were squeaks and a loud ruffling noise. Bats, disturbed by her sister's screams, began to pour out of the dark tunnel before them.

Horace swung Martha Rose out of the bats' path. Before the little girl reached the ground, he lost his footing and slipped. Martha Rose dropped her flashlight and it went out. Several yards ahead, Merry and Iris heard a thunk and a clattering of rocks, then silence.

Iris and Merry crouched together below the bats' flight path, clinging to one another.

"I want to go home," sobbed Merry.

"The bats are gone now," said Iris. "Daddy? Daddy?" There was no answer, only the dripping of water. "Martha Rose?" she called next. Iris trained her flashlight to the spot she had last seen her father and little sister.

Horace lay on his side, blood flowing from a gash on his head. Martha Rose was behind him, struggling to sit up.

"Daddy! Get off me! You squishin' my leg," she cried.

Iris and Merry crept over to them. Iris rolled her father off her little sister's leg.

"Owie, owie! My foot! I want Mama."

Iris turned to Merry. "You'll have to get help. Hurry home and get Mother. She'll be home now."

"Oh, no. I'm not going by myself," said Merry.

"You have to," said Iris.

"I can't! I can't! I'll get lost. You go, Iris," Merry wailed.

Iris jumped up. "Do you want to stay in this cave with Martha Rose and Daddy? You were paying attention to how we got here. You have to go. Look at Daddy." Iris trained her light on her father and then Merry. Tears streaked her sister's cheek.

Merry began to walk backwards to the cave's entrance. "I can't. I can't," she cried.

Iris gave her a push. "You can."

Martha Rose called, "Hurry up!"

Iris led Merry to the cave's mouth and watched as she began to run down the rocky hill at a dangerous speed. Her heart thumped as Merry almost fell. Iris watched her until she reached level ground and ran from sight.

As Iris returned to the cave, she heard her little sister screaming, "Iris! Iris!" She bent over and picked up the child, hugging her hard. Martha rose continued to cry, "I want Mama. I want Mama."

"I'm here. You're all right. Here, hold the flashlight. I'm going to look at Daddy." Iris sat her sister down and moved across the rocks to her motionless father. She sucked in her breath and held back tears as she placed her hands on his warm shirt. She felt his chest rise and fall. He was unconscious, but breathing.

She opened the canteen of water that had fallen off his shoulders. With a handkerchief she found in his shirt pocket, she sopped up the last of the water and wiped his head wound. It continued to bleed, so she held the cloth down hard, trying to stop the flow of dark red blood.

Iris remembered Oscar telling her how cold cave water was, and she wondered how far away the underground stream could be. The trickling noise sounded close.

She called out, "Martha Rose, I'm going just a little way down this path to see if I can find water."

"No! No! Don't you leave me!"

Iris backed away. "I'll hurry."

She aimed the flashlight so it made a path in front of her. She walked forward until the path turned to the left and listened. Yes. She did hear water nearby. The path curved left again; then there in her beam was a tiny stream that shone like silver. She filled the canteen with cold water and turned to retrace her steps.

How long had she been gone? She couldn't hear Martha Rose. Now the path curved right, once then twice, and she saw her father and sister on the floor. Martha Rose lay against his chest.

"I'm cold," she whimpered.

Iris knelt next to her father with the canteen. "Daddy?

116

Daddy?" she said as she held the cold handkerchief over his wound.

Martha Rose crawled close. "Iris? My foot hurts right here and I'm cold."

Iris looked at her sister's foot. Her ankle was swollen. She took off her sweater and wrapped around her sister. "Now that's the best I can do. We have to wait." She pulled Martha Rose close.

Iris kept her flashlight on. When she turned it off, darkness came down like a blanket. She hoped Merry would bring help fast. The rocky floor made it impossible to be comfortable, but Martha Rose, huddled in her lap, had fallen asleep.

The dripping and the trickling noise grew louder.

Occasionally her father groaned, and Iris trained the flashlight on his body.

Where was her sister? What if she got lost? She began to shiver. Suppose Merry fell and hurt herself! Would her father bleed to death? Iris shifted Martha Rose's weight and the little girl cried out in pain.

A clattering rock startled Iris. Could that be an animal? She told herself, *I will not scream.* She buried her face in her little sister's hair and closed her eyes.

Martha Rose woke up. "Iris, stop shaking me," she demanded. "Is you cryin'"?

"Yes."

"Is you scared?" Martha Rose's voice was full of wonder.

"Yes. Martha Rose, I have to get up. These rocks are killing me!"

"Are we goin' to get dead?"

"No. We are not. I'm going to move you so I can stand up. Help me so I won't hurt you."

Iris lifted the little girl onto the cave floor, stood and picked up Martha Rose in her arms and began to carry her towards the entrance of the cave.

"Where you takin' me?" asked her sister.

"I'm going to sit you in the sun at the entrance to the cave.

You can be the lookout and holler when you see people."

"Don't you leaf me." Martha Rose pinched Iris' arm hard.

"Hey! That hurts," yelled Iris.

"I'll pinch you hard if you leave me," said Martha Rose.

"I'm going back to Daddy," said Iris. She left her sister in the sun, walked away and entered the dark cave.

She heard Martha Rose shouting. Then her voice changed, "I see 'em! Iris, I see 'em!"

Iris returned to the mouth of the cave, waving and yelling to the approaching figures, "Hurry! Hurry!"

Laura Ellen was the first to crest the hill, sweaty and red-faced. She grabbed Iris' arm. "Where's your father?"

Iris' trembling increased and she pointed to the cave. "Just past the first curve."

Dr. Brenna was next and followed her mother inside.

Laughing Sky came last and grabbed Iris in her arms. She smoothed Iris' wild hair which had broken free of its ribbons and said, "It's going to be all right now. Men are coming with a stretcher. They will get your father to the hospital."

Dr. Brenna came blinking out of the cave and motioned for the men who were trudging up the hill to hurry. In minutes they carried Horace out of the cave on a stretcher. He already had a bandage on his head. Two straight poles supported one leg.

Laughing Sky instructed Iris to get the girls' things from the cave. "I can carry Martha Rose piggy-back," she said.

Iris turned to enter the cave and stepped back. "I can't go in," she gasped. "I can't."

Laughing Sky hugged her young friend. Guided by Iris' flashlight, she went into the cave to retrieve their bags.

Iris watched as the men maneuvered the canvas stretcher with her father's still form on it down the rocky hill. Her mother, white-faced, walked at his side.

*****

That evening as Laura Ellen and Iris sat by her father's hospital bed, Iris felt a gentle pressure on her hand. Her father opened his eyes. "Where's Martha Rose?"

He turned his head and saw his wife. "Laura Ellen?"

Iris' mother touched his cheek. "Oh, I should have gone with you. Why didn't I?" She began to cry.

"Mother," Iris said, "I always think it's my fault when Martha Rose gets hurt, yet you always tell me it would have happened anyway."

Horace said, "Iris, make your mother go home. I don't want either of you to feel like this is your fault." He closed his eyes. "Will Martha Rose ever forgive me for taking her into a cave full of bats? Where is she?"

"She has a sprained ankle but is soaking up the attention of our favorite nurse, Laughing Sky. We'd be lost without her help." Hesitantly Laura Ellen added, "You know what this means, don't you?"

Horace sighed and closed his eyes. "Yes. As soon as I started to fall, I thought in a flash: *This is it*!"

Iris jumped up, "Oh, Mother!"

Her mother gave her a sad smile. "We didn't get the blankets packed . . ."

Her father pointed to the plaster cast on his right leg and the turban of bandages around his head. "We can't stand to lose crops two years in a row. I wasn't meant to be a farmer. Iris, you will grow up a city girl." He shrank bank into his pillow. "It will be a blow to sell the farm." He closed his eyes.

Iris' mother pointed to the door and whispered, "We'll go and let him sleep."

They walked in silence out of the building. Laura Ellen wiped her eyes with her handkerchief before getting into the car.

"Mother, why were you going to pack blankets? Are we leaving? Had you already decided?" Iris asked.

Her mother cleared her throat. "Your father heard that his teaching position is still open. Last night we decided to go back to our little house. Now we'll wait to leave until after your father's head has begun to heal. Maybe go the second week of

September." Laura Ellen looked at her oldest child. "I'm sorry. I was beginning to believe we could do this."

Iris turned to her mother, "Oh, we can! I know we can!"

She had to strain to hear her mother's answer. "Your father is badly injured. It will be a long time before he can walk or work on the farm again."

Chapter Thirteen

AUGUST

Iris' father let out a yelp as she bumped his wheelchair out of the kitchen door to the car. Horace hoisted himself into the back seat and stretched his broken leg along it. Martha Rose cuddled next to him in his lap. "Come on," he said. "We'll be the wounded soldiers."

Merry asked, "What kind of a party is Laughing Sky having?"

Her father explained. "There's an annual August picnic. The whole town comes. Last year we missed it by a week."

Iris was quiet. She knew the news her parents would share with her sisters when they got home. It would cancel any fun there might be today. Dr. Brenna insisted that her father needed rest. His head injury still left him woozy, and his broken leg would take time to heal. Iris' mother and father were set on going back to Virginia. Her sisters didn't know.

When Martha Rose was settled, Iris wrestled the wheelchair into the trunk of the car and slammed it shut. Iris and Merry sat in the front seat with their mother at the wheel. Her mother drove past ripe grain fields, oats and wheat shining in the sun. She noticed her mother look at her father in the rear view mirror, catch his eye, then look quickly away at the road. Last year's crop was a disaster. This year's was terrific.

Iris' confidence was shattered by the cave ordeal. The silence after her father's fall had been unbearable. She thought he was dead. She remembered Oscar sobbing in his kitchen when his father was injured in February. She trembled when she thought of that day. She was equally scared in the cave. Both she and Oscar thought they had lost their fathers. And Laughing Sky had called her The Bold One. Iris guessed she'd need a new name.

121

When her mother pulled the car to a stop beside Laughing Sky's cabin, Iris saw her friend on the porch. When she stood up, all three girls gaped.

Martha Rose shouted. "She got on all her In-di-an clothes!" One Deer was there too in traditional Ojibway dress. A necklace of porcupine quills and bear teeth hung on his chest. Martha Rose hopped from the car and limped towards him. "Where'd you get those teef?" she asked.

One Deer swooped her into his arms and hugged her. "Hello, little sister," he said. "Welcome to the party." He hurried to the car and assisted Horace into the wheelchair. "Mr. Anderson, we are happy to see you!"

Iris pushed One Deer aside and maneuvered her father's chair over the uneven ground. Laura Ellen walked beside them and murmured, "My heart is not in this."

Horace looked up at his wife and nodded in agreement.

Iris muttered, "Then why are we here?"

Laughing Sky came down the steps in a deer skin skirt with a fringed hem and seams. She wore beaded moccasins on her feet, and her glossy hair hung in braids over her shoulders. Iris said to her, "This is the most beautiful I have ever seen you!"

"That is because this is who I am." She turned so Iris could get the whole picture of her outfit.

The yard beside the cabin was full of people. Long tables from church were set out and covered with cloths and dishes of food. Iris saw Julie and her parents and waved. Julie came over and examined Martha Rose's wrapped ankle.

"It really hurts bad," said the little girl. "Look, I can't hardly walk." She limped as though she were walking on hot coals which got a laugh from Julie's father. "It was swole up this big," she held her hands the size of a cantaloupe.

Iris shook her head. "Martha Rose is the queen of exaggeration."

Julie laughed and said, "I wish I had a little sister like Martha Rose. She makes everybody laugh."

The postmaster and his wife Ruth were there with their five

boys, also Pastor and Mrs. Nilsen and Mr. Burmeister from the carpentry shop with his new wife Jacqueline. Mr. Halker and his wife had their baby girl with them. They lived over the grocery store Mr. Halker owned.

Iris looked around for Oscar and his father. She didn't see them, but there was an Indian pony much like Blue tied to a tree near the edge of the circle. It was brown and white with a white mane and tail. Iris left her family and she and Julie went up to the pony, who let her stroke her neck. "Julie, do you know whose pony this is?" Iris asked.

Julie said, "I've never seen this horse."

"What a beautiful animal you are," said Iris. "I wish I could get on you and ride away. Right now. Anywhere!" She rubbed the horse's forehead with her knuckles.

Julie looked at her friend and said, "Oh, I wish you wouldn't say that! I'd miss you so!"

One Deer came up to them. "This is War Bonnet," he said.

"Is she yours?" asked Iris. "She's an Indian pony, isn't she?"

"She is," he answered. Then he stooped over, put his hands on his knees and looked at Iris. "I am going to give up a secret. Can you keep it?"

"Oh, yes," answered Iris.

He looked at Julie.

"Of course," she replied.

"Iris, she's yours," he said. "She needs to be ridden. She also needs a barn and attention. I'm going to Canada in September for a year on another reservation. I'll be driving dogsleds and tracking. She's yours for keeps."

"You can't leave now," whispered Julie to Iris, her brown eyes as bright as creek rocks.

Iris looked at the ground, tears forming in the corner of her eyes. Panic filled her voice, "Well, you don't understand, One Deer. We have a secret too . . . . my family . . . I can't . . . . I can't take her . . . You see. . ."

One Deer interrupted, "Iris, things will be different in a few weeks. Listen, do you know how proud my sister is of you? How brave you were in that cave! You stayed with your father. You comforted Martha Rose. You sent Merry to get help. You must have been terrified. Do you believe that everything that has happened this year happened for nothing? This pony is yours. Believe me. All *is* going to be well."

Laughing Sky stood on the porch, clapping her hands. Martha Rose leaned next to her. Everyone stood and listened, "Martha Rose, I have a basket for you."

There was a picnic basket with a dish towel over it. Martha Rose peeked under it. "Kitties!" she cried. "Boys or girls?"

Laughing Sky answered, "Two girls."

"This one Muffin and this one Biscuit, 'cause I like them," said Martha Rose.

Horace spoke up, "Hmm, we have Cookie the puppy, now Muffin and Biscuit. My little girl has a one-track mind."

Mr. Halker walked up the steps to the porch next and called Merry to join him. Laughing Sky came around the side of the cabin with a lamb no bigger than a teddy bear in her arms. Merry's eyes widened.

Mr. Halker took the lamb from Laughing Sky and handed it to Merry. "Merry, will you take this lamb? She was orphaned by her mother, and I think you would be just the person to bottle feed her. You have the patience for it. Yes, I do believe you do. You know, we have our own baby to take care of this fall."

Merry stood there with the cuddly white lamb in her arms. Iris had never seen that look on her face. Merry was beyond happy.

Iris looked for her mother's and father's reactions. Her father's head was bowed, but her mother looked right at her. Things were getting out of hand. They should have stayed home. She left Julie and the pony and went to stand next to her mother. Maybe they should leave.

Merry continued to beam and told Mr. Halker, "This is Snowball."

"I can tell he's found a good home," he said.

Pastor Nilsen walked up the steps and cleared his throat.

"Speech! Speech!" cried some of the men.

He held up his hand for silence. "Friends and dear neighbors, these gifts to the Andersen girls are our way of celebrating their first year in the Andersen house."

Cheers of "Hurray! Hurray!" filled the air.

Laura Ellen gave the pastor a long mean look.

Pastor Nilsen added, "One Deer, please say grace."

The group grew quiet as One Deer raised his hands, palms up and began, "Grandfather, Great Spirit, the hearts of your people are alike. Look upon the Andersen family so they may face the winds of change boldly. Be with us as we work and play together until we walk the road to the Day of Quiet Rest. Give us strength to understand that when life is hard, You give us eyes to see Your love. Bless our crops and the animals who give their lives so that we might survive on Your good earth. Teach us to walk here as relatives to all that live here. Amen."

Pastor Nilsen said, "Amen indeed. Now let us feast!"

Iris watched Merry fill her plate with corn on the cob, fried trout, rolls and potato salad. Iris thought that if she ate anything, it would stick in her throat.

Her father was shaking hands and seemed full of good spirits. She wondered how he could keep it up. Her mother brought him a plate of food and he declared, "Food always tastes best outdoors." He was putting on a good act. Horace looked around at the gathering. "Laughing Sky, where are Earl and Oscar, and where's Trig?" he asked.

"They had extra chores. I'm sure they are on their way," she explained.

After September's tornado, Earl and Trig Gundersen had helped Horace get in his disastrous crop. The men worked together on each other's farms to salvage what they could. Iris' father wouldn't be able to help anyone else for a long time.

She took up a wheat roll to nibble. A pickup truck came down the road, spinning dust behind it.

"Here they are," said Laughing Sky. "I'll get another pitcher of lemonade."

Trig, Earl and Oscar got out of the truck and brushed dirt and chaff from their overalls. Trig came over and shook Horace's hand, "Glad to see you out of the house, Horace."

Horace called to Earl and Oscar, "We left you a little food."

Oscar came over to Iris, but she couldn't look him in the face. "Hi," he said.

Iris hung her head and sighed.

Pastor Nilsen spoke from the steps. "Now, Laura Ellen, Horace, girls, our hearts are full of secret merriment." He came down the steps and put his hand on Horace's shoulder and looked Laura Ellen in the eye.

"Listen well . . . Harmony is a small town. People get to be more than friends. They become family and share good times like we're doing today." He looked around at the gathering. "They share difficult times too. After a year in Harmony, you are our family. Today Trig, Earl and Oscar began to harvest your excellent corn crop, Horace. Your bones and bruises will heal, and one day you can repay someone else with your own labor. We want you and your good family to continue to be a part of our lives."

Earl spoke up in his quiet voice, "This community will not give up. Our family knows that."

It was the most Iris had ever heard him say at one time.

Laughing Sky added, "Laura Ellen, you followed your husband to this difficult strange place. All of these friends will help you. And . . . soon a new Andersen will sleep in the family cradle. Am I right?" She smiled at the woman who stood next to her husband's wheelchair.

"Well, yes . . . yes, you are," said Laura Ellen, as she took the handkerchief Horace offered her.

"What cradle?" asked Merry.

"The one in the attic," said Iris. "I saw it there. Martha Rose was there, and she said, 'This is for brother,' but I didn't think anything of it."

Laura Ellen announced to her husband, "Horace, there will be a baby in it in February. Your injury and Martha Rose's took the air out of me too. I was waiting to tell you." She took his hand and said, "We're going to have a baby right here in Harmony."

"We are talkin' 'bout babies," said Martha Rose, grinning.

"Yes!" hollered Iris. "This means we're staying?"

Martha Rose began to skip around the circle of listeners and sing, "Benjamin! Benjamin!"

Iris leaned over her father's wheelchair and repeated, "This means we're staying?"

He looked at the small group gathered around. He waved his arms around, "All this means we're staying."

Horace looked up at his wife, then at his oldest daughter, and took her face in his two hands, said, "We are!"

*****

Dusk settled and fireflies began to blink in the grass. Lanterns were brought out and laughter filled the evening. Oscar admired Iris' pony. As she patted War Bonnet, he covered her hand with his. "I knew you would stay," he said. "It couldn't have happened any other way."

Julie hugged Iris so hard that Iris could feel her friend's bones.

Julie was crying. "Oh, my friend, my best friend ever! Oh, Iris!"

As the deep purple night cooled, guests began to drift home. The name "Benjamin, Benjamin," sung by Martha Rose, echoed and carried all the way to the river and the caves where the dripping of water went unnoticed. The vines at the mouth of the dark entrance swayed in the breeze.